GINA'S
LITTLE SECRET

BY
JENNIFER TAYLOR

MILLS
BOON®

First published in Great Britain 2012
by Mills & Boon, an imprint of Harlequin (UK) Limited.
Large Print edition 2012
Harlequin (UK) Limited, Eton House,
18-24 Paradise Road, Richmond, Surrey TW9 1SR

© Jennifer Taylor 2012

ISBN: 978 0 263 22466 5

Printed and bound in Great Britain
by CPI Antony Rowe, Chippenham, Wiltshire

'I have remembered, Gina.'

Gina paused uncertainly. 'Remembered?'

'*Si.* Oh, I can't recall everything that happened between us, but I know that we were close at one point.'

His voice dropped, and she shivered when she felt the richly accented tones stroking along her nerves.

'We were lovers, weren't we?'

'I…' She had to stop and swallow to unlock the knot in her throat. She was tempted to deny the allegation, but what was the point if Marco had remembered? 'Yes, we were.'

'I thought so. I remember us being in a café overlooking the River Arno. It was a cold day and you were wearing my scarf. *Si?*'

Heat flowed through her as she instantly recalled the occasion. When they had stopped for coffee, and he had leaned across the table and kissed her, she had known her life would never be the same again. That was the moment when she had realised that she was in love with him—the moment when she had felt that all her dreams were about to come true.

Pain seared through her. It was all she could do not to cry out, but she couldn't afford to let him know how much he had hurt her. If she could pass off their relationship as little more than a brief affair then he would stop digging for information and Lily would be safe.

Jennifer Taylor lives in the north-west of England, in a small village surrounded by some really beautiful countryside. She has written for several different Mills & Boon® series in the past, but it wasn't until she read her first Medical™ Romance that she truly found her niche. She was so captivated by these heart-warming stories that she set out to write them herself! When she's not writing, or doing research for her latest book, Jennifer's hobbies include reading, gardening, travel, and chatting to friends both on and off-line. She is always delighted to hear from readers, so do visit her website at www.jennifer-taylor.com

Recent titles by the same author:

SMALL TOWN MARRIAGE MIRACLE
THE MIDWIFE'S CHRISTMAS MIRACLE
THE DOCTOR'S BABY BOMBSHELL*
THE GP'S MEANT-TO-BE BRIDE*
MARRYING THE RUNAWAY BRIDE*
THE SURGEON'S FATHERHOOD SURPRISE**

*Dalverston Weddings
**Brides of Penhally Bay*

**These titles are also available in ebook format
from www.millsandboon.co.uk**

To Pam and Dudley, with love and thanks for all your help and support.

CHAPTER ONE

4 p.m. 11 December

'THAT was ED on the phone. Bet you can't guess what they wanted?'

Sister Georgina Lee groaned as she looked up from the computer. 'Don't tell me—they want us to find yet *another* bed for yet *another* patient.'

'Got it in one!' Rosie James, their young student nurse, grinned. 'Give yourself a pat on the back.'

'I would do if I had the time to spare.' Gina's expression was wry as she glanced at the computer screen. 'It's the third time I've tried to fill in this order form. At this rate, we're going to run out of basic supplies.'

'It has been busy,' Rosie agreed. 'I had no idea that life on the acute assessment unit would be so hectic. I thought it would be a doddle, to be honest. Patients would be sent here for a couple of hours and then they'd either be moved to a ward or sent home.'

'That's what most folk believe if they haven't worked here.' Gina laughed, her slate-grey eyes filled with amusement. 'It's what I thought happened here too when I took this job. I soon discovered how wrong I was!'

'It must have been a shock,' Rosie suggested.

Gina shrugged. 'A bit, but I must admit that I enjoy the variety. If you work on a ward like Women's Surgical, for instance, then you know that your patients will be either preparing for an operation or recovering from one. In here, you never know what you're going to have to deal with. It certainly keeps you on your toes.'

'I suppose so, although I'm not sure I'd be able to cope with the pressure, long term,' Rosie admitted.

'It's not for everyone,' Gina said firmly, not wanting the younger woman to feel discouraged. She shot another glance at the screen and stood up. 'We'd better go and see if we can sort out a bed. Mr Walker in the end bay is supposed to be moving to Cardiology, so maybe we can sweet-talk them into taking him sooner than planned.'

Gina led the way, pausing en route to let the rest of the staff know that another admission was on the way. She smiled when her friend, Julie Grey, groaned. 'I know how you feel, Jules. We're bursting at the seams as it is. At this rate we'll soon be having to use the staffroom!'

'Either that or leave patients on trolleys in the corridor as used to happen in the past,' Julie said ruefully.

'Thank heavens those days are gone,' Gina retorted. 'The thought of any patient being abandoned like that makes my blood run cold.'

'We all hated it,' Julie assured her. 'This new unit might get crowded but it's a huge improvement on how things used to be.'

Gina left the staff to get on with their work and went to have a word with Frank Walker. He had been rushed in by ambulance at lunchtime complaining of chest pains. Subsequent tests had shown blockages to three of the main coronary arteries and the decision had been made to perform a bypass. Now Gina smiled as she stopped beside his bed.

'So how are you feeling now, Mr Walker?'

'So-so. The pain has eased off thanks to the medication, so that's a blessing.' He sighed. 'I suppose I've only got myself to blame. My wife's been nagging me for years to stop smoking and eat sensibly but I took no notice. I thought she was making a fuss about nothing.'

'It's hard to accept advice sometimes,' Gina said tactfully. 'Still, once you've had the bypass done, you'll feel a lot better.'

'Do you think so?' Frank looked worried. 'Oh, I know that young chap who came to see me was very dismissive, but you can't help worrying, can you? I mean, they have to stop your heart and everything.'

'Yes, they do, but they attach you to a special machine which takes over the jobs your heart and lungs would normally do,' Gina explained, wishing, not for the first time, that Miles Humphreys had a better bedside manner. An operation such as this might be routine to him but it certainly wasn't routine for the patient.

'So you think it's quite safe, do you, Sister?' Frank said anxiously. 'And that I should have it done?'

'I do. Although it's a major operation, it's performed frequently. And I know for a fact that the cardio team here at St Saviour's are highly skilled.' She patted Frank's hand. 'You'll be fine, I promise you.'

'Thank you.' Frank smiled at her. 'I feel much happier now. Shame that young doctor didn't take the time to reassure me like you've just done. You should give him a few tips on how to talk to his patients.'

Gina smiled although she didn't say anything. Talking to Miles was something she was trying to avoid. Ever since he'd asked her out on a date and she'd refused, there'd been an atmosphere when he came into the ward. If only he would accept that there was nothing personal about her refusing his invitation.

She sighed as she went to phone the cardiology unit. The truth was she wasn't interested in Miles or any other man. She'd had her heart broken once and there was no way that she was going to risk it happening again, especially when it could impact on Lily. Making sure that her two-year-old daughter was safe and happy was all that mattered. There was no room in her life for a relationship.

Frank Walker had just been transferred to the cardiology unit when the porters arrived with their latest admission. Gina was in the office, making yet another attempt to get to grips with the paperwork, but she went out to meet them. Julie had already directed them to the end bay and they were manoeuvring the bed into place when Gina got there.

'So, who have we got?' she asked, unclipping the notes from the foot rail. She glanced at the patient's details. Name: Marco Andretti. Age: thirty-seven. Address: Villa Rosa, Florence, Italy. Just for a moment the full impact of what she was reading didn't hit her and then all of a sudden her heart began to pound. It had to be a mistake! It couldn't be her Marco....

Could it?

Gina took a deep breath as she forced herself to look at the man lying on the bed. His eyes were shut and the right side of his head was swathed in a thick white dressing but neither of those things mattered. As her eyes drank in the olive-tanned skin, the elegant nose, the chiselled jaw and sensuous curve of his mouth she felt panic assail her. It *was* Marco. There was no mistake about that!

'Gina? Hey, are you OK?'

Gina jumped when Julie tapped her on the arm. She knew there was no point claiming that she was fine because her friend wouldn't believe her. 'I...um...I feel a bit queasy, that's all. I expect I'm hungry.'

'Probably because you worked straight through your break.' Julie made flapping movements with her hands. 'Go on, scoot! You go and make yourself a cup of coffee. We can manage here, can't we, Rosie?'

'Well, if you're sure...' Gina turned away when

the older woman nodded. Normally, she wouldn't have dreamt of leaving the staff to settle in a new patient without her being present, but this wasn't a normal situation, was it? A wave of hysterical laughter welled up inside her and she pressed her hand to her mouth as she made her way to the staffroom. Thankfully, there was nobody in there so she switched on the kettle then sank down on a chair as her legs suddenly gave way.

What twist of fate had brought Marco here to the very hospital where she worked? she wondered dizzily. It would be three years this Christmas since she had seen him last, three whole years since he had told her bluntly that he didn't envisage them ever having a future together. His expression had been so cold that any protests she might have made had remained unuttered. What would have been the point of trying to convince him that they'd had something special, something worth fighting for, when he obviously hadn't believed that himself? She couldn't have *made* him love her, definitely wouldn't have begged him to, so she had done what he had wanted and walked away.

Gina's heart was heavy as she recalled that terrible period in her life. She had wondered in the beginning if once she had gone, he might realise that he missed her more than he had thought; however, as the weeks had passed, and he had made no attempt to contact her, she had accepted how foolish she'd been to hope for that. Marco may have enjoyed making love to her. He may even have enjoyed spending time with her for a short while, but he had never needed her as a permanent part of his life.

It had been hard to face that fact but at least it had made it easier to decide what to do when Lily was born. But now Marco was here and Gina knew that his reappearance in her life would have repercussions. It was bound to. Marco was Lily's father. He had a daughter he knew nothing about.

CHAPTER TWO

'RIGHT, everything's sorted. One of the neuro team will be here shortly... Hello! Earth to Gina—are you receiving me?'

'What?' Gina jumped when Julie appeared in front of her. She took a quick breath, forcing the feeling of panic to retreat if not to actually disappear. The situation was way too volatile to hope that would happen.

'Sorry, I was miles away,' she said, getting up to spoon instant coffee into a couple of mugs. She added boiling water then reached for the sugar jar, deriving comfort from the familiar routine. Maybe that was the answer, she thought suddenly. Behave normally and Marco wouldn't suspect anything was wrong. After all, there was no reason to tell him about Lily, was there?

'Here, let me do that. I know I like my coffee sweet but three spoons of sugar is too much even for me!' Julie edged her aside, tipping the offending brew down the sink before starting again from scratch. She treated Gina to an old-fashioned look as she handed her a fresh mug of coffee. 'If I didn't know better, I'd say the sight of our dishy new patient has knocked you for six.'

'Rubbish!' Gina gave a sharp little laugh, anxious to stamp on that idea before it could take hold. The last thing she needed was people speculating. 'I'm just hungry, as I said. I didn't have time to eat anything before I came into work, so it's my own fault.'

'I've got some sandwiches left. Here you go.' Julie handed her a plastic container then leant against the work top while she drank her coffee.

'Thanks.' Gina forced herself to bite into one of the thick ham sandwiches even though the last thing she felt like doing was eating. Could she pull it off, make sure that Marco remained unaware of Lily's existence? After all, he would only be in AAU for a short while; he would either be moved to a ward or discharged depending on what treatment he required. There was no reason why she should bring up the subject of their daughter.

Pain speared through her and she hurriedly took another bite of the sandwich. Their daughter, the child they had conceived together. She had truly believed that they had been making love when it must have happened, but that wasn't how Marco had viewed it. It couldn't have been. It had just been sex for him, pure and simple, and the fact that it had resulted in a beautiful, healthy little girl was incidental.

'I've not dealt with a case like this before. It's one of those things you read about but rarely experience.'

Gina looked up when she realised that once again her thoughts had been running off at a tangent. 'What do you mean?'

'Amnesia. Hopefully, he'll recover his memory soon, but it must be really scary, not knowing who you are.'

'You're talking about Marco?' Gina queried, then flushed when Julie looked at her in surprise.

'That is his name, isn't it? I think that's what it said in his notes.'

'Yes, that's right. Marco Andretti. Apparently he's a doctor, a trauma specialist, no less. I don't know if that makes it better or worse, do you?'

'I've no idea,' Gina replied, struggling to follow what her friend was saying. 'Are you telling me that he's lost his memory?'

'Hmm. Seems he had no idea who he was or where he was going when he was brought into ED. All the paramedics could tell them was that he was on his way from Heathrow when he was involved in an RTA.'

'So how did they find out his name?'

'One of the staff went through his pockets and found his passport—they got the details from that. They also found a letter confirming the time and date of an interview for the post of Head of Trauma care at the Southern Free. He must be pretty high up the ladder if he's being interviewed for a post like that.' Julie grimaced. 'Not that it helps very much at the moment. It must be awful for him, mustn't it? He's all on his own in a strange country and he hasn't got a clue who he is.'

'So what's going to happen next?' Gina asked, her head reeling from what she had learned. Marco had come to London to attend an interview? She had never imagined that he would leave Italy and the news threw her so that it was hard to concentrate when Julie continued.

'The police are going to try to contact his family. I expect he's married. I can't imagine a gorgeous hunk like him being single, can you? Hopefully, his wife will be able to fly over to be with him. One thing's certain, though—he's going to need a lot of support until he gets his memory back.'

Gina put the sandwich down after Julie left. Standing up, she went to the door. She could just see the end bay from where she stood although she couldn't see the man who was lying in the bed there. So Marco had lost his memory? He didn't remember who he was or anything about his life? She too had read about this kind of thing happening, but had never experienced it. Would he remember her? she wondered suddenly.

Her heart began to race. In one way it would be so much easier if he had forgotten about her, yet in another she couldn't bear to think that those few weeks they'd spent together might have been expunged from his mind forever. Even though it was crazy to feel like this, she knew she had to find out.

She closed the staffroom door and made her way back to the ward. Everything was starting to settle down now as the patients adjusted to the idea that they were in hospital. There was open visiting in AAU and there were a number of friends and relatives gathered around the beds, but even they seemed calmer. It was always a shock when a loved one was rushed into hospital and people reacted in many different ways to the stress.

Gina had learned to cope with it all, the anger, the fear, the questions. It was rare that anything fazed her but she had to admit that her nerves were jangling as she approached the end bay.

Marco still had his eyes closed and didn't seem aware of her presence as she stood beside the bed, looking down at him. He had always been an extremely handsome man and nothing had changed in that respect. His body looked as lean and fit as ever beneath the thin hospital gown, his skin glowed with good health, his dark hair was lustrous and thick. Only the few strands of grey at his temples proved that time had passed, but even they did little to detract from his appeal.

Gina felt her stomach muscles clench as a wave of awareness rushed through her. Despite everything Marco had said and done three years ago, despite how much he had hurt her, she was still attracted to him!

Marco could feel the blood pounding inside his skull. He knew it was a result of the accident because the ED consultant had explained it to him. When the car he had been travelling in had collided with a lorry that had pulled out in front of them, he had hit his head and suffered a concussion. That accounted for the headache but did it really explain why he couldn't remember who he was or where he'd been going?

He opened his eyes, gripping hold of the rails at the sides of the bed when the room swam sickeningly. Taking a deep breath, he forced the nausea to subside and focused on his surroundings. White walls, blue curtains, a familiar smell of antiseptic, which all added up to his being in hospital. He knew where he was. He also knew that it was somewhere he was used to being, too.

Marco frowned as he tried to make sense of that idea. Had he been ill recently, so ill that he had needed a prolonged stay in hospital? He didn't think so. Apart from the headache, he felt quite well, not like someone who was recovering from an illness. So if he hadn't been a patient, had he worked in a hospital in some capacity?

That idea seemed much more fitting. He closed his eyes again as he let it seep into his consciousness. He worked in a hospital? Yes, that was right. He knew instinctively it was true. And yet there was something odd about being here, something not related to the fact that normally he wouldn't be lying in bed...

It was the voices, he realised with a start. Or, more accurately, the fact that they were speaking English. Although he understood what was being said, he knew that English wasn't his first language. What was?

'Dr Andretti. Can you hear me?'

Marco's eyes shot open when a quiet voice spoke beside him. Turning his head, he saw a nurse standing beside the bed. She was small and blonde, her hair caught back at the nape of her neck with a dark blue ribbon that matched the blue of her uniform. Marco felt something stir inside him, something that felt almost like recognition. He had the strangest feeling that he had seen her before, but before he could work out where, she spoke again.

'How do you feel?'

Her voice was soft, husky, and Marco felt a ripple of awareness run through him. The low, sweet tone of her voice was oddly soothing as it flowed along his taut nerves. For the first time since he had regained consciousness in the back of the ambulance he didn't feel afraid.

'I am not sure.' His own voice sounded rough and he paused while he tried to work some moisture into his mouth. The nurse must have realised his dilemma because she reached for the jug and filled a glass with water. Bending, she slid her hand beneath his head and raised it a fraction while she held the glass to his lips.

'Take a sip of this,' she instructed, tilting the glass so that a trickle of cool water slid between his lips.

Marco swallowed greedily, frowning when she took the glass away, and she smiled faintly, her grey eyes filled with understanding. 'You'll be sick if you drink too much. You can have another sip in a moment.'

She gently removed her hand and he felt a wave of disappointment wash over him that owed nothing to the fact that he'd been deprived of the water. Why should it have felt so good to have her touch him like that? he wondered. And why did he want her to touch him again?

He watched as she placed the glass on the bedside cabinet, studying the gentle curve of her cheek, the sweeping length of her lashes, the upward tilt of her small nose. She was extremely pretty in a very English way with that fine, pale skin and those delicate features. Everything about her was refined, feminine, and he found it very appealing. He realised with a start that he was attracted to her, even though she was very different in appearance from Francesca.

The memory slid into his mind without any warning. He remembered who Francesca was, how she had looked...*everything*! Pain lanced through him and he closed his eyes, wondering if he could bear to go through the agony all over again. If this was what it felt like to get his memory back, he would rather forget!

Gina frowned as she looked down at Marco. His eyes were tightly shut and his hands were clenched into fists. Bending, she felt for his pulse, concerned in case he had taken a sudden turn for the worse. Head injuries were notoriously difficult to treat and it wasn't unknown for a patient's condition to deteriorate in the blink of an eye.

The thought sent a shaft of fear scudding through her. Gina's fingers tightened around his wrist as she counted the life-giving beats. Julie should have put him on a monitor, she thought as she made a rapid calculation. He needed his blood pressure checked and his oxygen saturation levels monitored. You really couldn't take any chances with an injury like this.

His eyes suddenly opened and she felt her own blood pressure zoom several notches up the scale when she found herself staring into their golden-brown depths. Was that recognition she could see in his gaze? Had Marco remembered who she was? The thought scared her and she let his hand drop back onto the bed, afraid that her touch would be the catalyst to make him regain his memory. She didn't want that to happen until she had worked out what she should do about Lily!

'I'd be happier if you were on a monitor,' she said hurriedly, ashamed that she could think that way. It must be terrible for Marco to lose his memory and she should be doing everything she could to help him…

Everything except telling him about Lily and how the little girl had been conceived, a small voice whispered inside her head.

'Just lie there and try to relax while I fetch it,' she instructed as calmly as she could. She hurried away, afraid that he would realise something was wrong if she lingered. There was a spare monitor outside the office so she went to fetch it then hesitated, unsure if she should go back at that moment. Although she wanted him to recover his memory, maybe it would be better if she steered clear. He would be going up to Neurology soon and once he left AAU that would be the last she needed to see of him. When Rosie appeared, she called her over.

'Can you set this up in the end bay for Dr Andretti? I want you to keep an eye on him, too. Don't let him go to sleep. We need to check there's nothing brewing.'

'But ED said he was OK,' Rosie protested. 'He's had a CT scan and it was clear.'

'That may be so, but it isn't unknown for a bleed to develop later,' Gina said sharply. 'That's why he's been sent here, so we can monitor what's happening.'

'Oh, I see. Sorry. I just assumed he was here because of losing his memory.' Rosie looked so downcast that Gina instantly regretted being so brusque with her.

'That's certainly one of the reasons why he was sent to us, I imagine. Hopefully, someone from the neuro team will be here soon. I'll give them a call and see what's happening. But in the meantime, we'll apply both belt and braces, i.e. put him on a monitor *and* do fifteen-minute obs.'

'I understand.' Rosie perked up a bit. She grinned as she manoeuvred the monitor out of the corner. 'Not that it's any hardship to keep an eye on him, mind. He's definitely fit, *despite* his age!'

Gina laughed as the young nurse hurried away. Anyone would think that Marco was in his dotage if they heard that, whereas from what she had seen, he was in his prime. Her heart gave a little jolt at the thought and she hurried into the office to phone Neurology. They promised to send someone down within the hour so she had to leave it at that. There were other patients who needed her attention, after all; she couldn't devote herself solely to Marco's care even if she wanted to, which she didn't.

She squared her shoulders. Marco had made his feelings perfectly clear three years ago and even though he may have lost his memory, she doubted if he had changed his mind. She hadn't figured in his life back then and she wouldn't figure in it now, with or without Lily.

CHAPTER THREE

BY THE time the neuro registrar arrived, Marco was feeling decidedly out of sorts. It seemed that every time he closed his eyes that young nurse would appear and start talking to him. He was sick and tired of her shrill little voice buzzing in his ears like a demented wasp. Why hadn't that other nurse come back, he thought impatiently, the one who had spoken to him so gently? He could put up with her disturbing him very easily.

He frowned as once again a memory tried to surface only to disappear the moment he attempted to capture it. He was more convinced than ever that he had met her before, but if that were the case then why hadn't she said something? His head ached even more as he tried to work it out but it was just too difficult. Hopefully, it would all come back to him in time, all the good memories as well as the bad, like those about Francesca.

Sadness welled up inside him and he closed his eyes, afraid that in his present state he would do something unforgivable like cry. After Francesca had died, he hadn't cried, hadn't been able to. He had been too numb at first, too eaten up by grief later to give vent to his emotions. Over the years it had become increasingly important that he shouldn't break down. He had needed to remain strong if he was to stick to his decision never to allow himself to fall in love again. There had been just that one time he had wavered, when he had realised that he was letting himself feel things he shouldn't…

'Dr Andretti? I'm Steven Pierce, the neuro registrar. Sorry about the delay but it's been like a madhouse today.'

The memory melted away and Marco's eyes shot open. He stared at the man standing beside the bed then let his gaze move to the woman beside him. So she was back, was she? She had deigned to spare him some time now that her colleague had decided to pay him a visit?

Marco's irritation levels shot up several notches and he glared at the younger man. 'About time too. Is it normal practice to leave a patient suffering from a head trauma in a busy ward like this?' His gaze skimmed around the room, taking stock of the patients and their visitors, and his expression was frosty when he looked at the nurse. 'The noise level in here is appalling, Sister. If I was in charge of this department then you can be sure that it would be run along very different lines.'

'But you aren't in charge, are you, Dr Andretti?'

Her voice was still soft, but there was a coolness about it that stung and Marco's frown deepened. However, before he could say anything else the younger doctor intervened.

'Unfortunately, AAU is one of the busiest departments in the hospital. We think we have a tough time on the wards, but I don't know how the staff here copes with all the comings and goings.'

Marco inclined his head, acknowledging the rebuke and the justification for it. He had been rude and there was no excuse for that. 'Of course. I apologise if my comments caused offence, Sister. *Mi scusi.*'

'There is nothing to apologise for.'

Her tone was still chilly and he felt a prickle of disappointment nibble away at his irritation. For some reason he couldn't explain, he didn't want her to be so distant with him. The thought surprised him so that it was a moment before he realised the registrar was speaking again.

'I noticed that you spoke Italian just now, Dr Andretti. Obviously, some aspects of your life are starting to return.'

'Si,' he concurred slowly. 'I realised earlier that English wasn't my first language, but it is only now that I know Italian is.'

Steven Pierce nodded. 'It's a start. You will probably find that bits and pieces come back to you in no particular order. You'll recall one event and not recall something else that happened at the same time.'

'You think it is retrograde amnesia,' Marco queried.

'Yes, more than likely. Most people with amnesia suffer a gap in their memory that extends backwards from the onset of the disorder. When you hit your head during the accident that was the start and now you're finding it difficult to recall what went on before then.' Steven smiled. 'However, the fact that you are able to diagnose your own condition is another indication that your memory is starting to return.'

'*Bene.* It is not pleasant to not know who you are and what has happened to you,' Marco admitted. He glanced at the nurse and felt surprise run through him when he saw the alarm on her face. It was obvious that something was troubling her even though she was doing her best to disguise it.

She must have sensed he was looking at her because she glanced round and he saw the colour run up her face before she turned away, busying herself with rearranging the water jug and glass. Marco knew that it was merely an excuse to avoid looking at him and felt more perplexed than ever.

It was on the tip of his tongue to ask her what was wrong when the younger man continued.

'I'd like to move you to the neuro unit so we can run some tests, but unfortunately we're short of beds right now.' He turned to the nurse. 'I'm afraid Dr Andretti will have to stay here for to-night, Gina. Sorry about that.'

'It's fine. Don't worry about it.'

She summoned a smile but Marco could tell how strained it was even if the other man didn't appear to notice. He listened without interrupting while the registrar explained that he would like Marco to be kept under observation. If he was honest, his attention was focused more on Gina than on the plans for his ongoing care.

Marco shivered as he silently repeated the name. Once again there was that flash of recognition, the feeling that he had met her before. He tried to force the fog from his brain but it wouldn't lift. Was he imagining it? Was his brain trying to compensate for its lack of memories by creating new ones?

As a doctor, he knew it was possible. False

memories could be implanted in a person's mind; it was a proven fact. But why would he want to do such a thing? Surely he wasn't so desperate to ease his loneliness that he would choose to latch onto a total stranger?

That was another memory, the fact that he was lonely. Marco let it settle in his mind then dismissed it as he did every single time. He wouldn't allow himself to wish for more than he had. He'd had everything a man could have dreamed of once and lost it. He couldn't and wouldn't go through that agony again.

His heart began to pound as he looked at the woman standing beside the bed. Maybe he couldn't recall where they had met but he knew— *he just knew*—that they had! In that second he realised how vital it was that he regain his memory as quickly as possible. He had to find out why Gina was pretending not to know him.

The evening wore on, bringing with it the usual mix of the mundane and high drama. Gina had worked on AAU for almost two years and had seen it all before, but that night seemed very different from all the others. She was so conscious of Marco's presence that her senses seemed acutely heightened. The noise level *was* extremely high; the number of visitors per bed *did* need reducing; waiting times *were* too long—people needed to be seen by a specialist far sooner than was currently happening.

She sent Julie off to clear the ward of excess visitors. Two per bed was the designated limit and she intended to stick to that. While Julie was doing that, she phoned all the departments that were supposed to be sending someone down to see a patient, refusing to accept the usual excuse that they were short of staff. As she politely reminded them, AAU was for acute cases only. It wasn't an overflow for the various wards. She had just finished when she heard a monitor beeping and Rosie came rushing into the office.

'The man in bed seven can't breathe!' the student gabbled at her.

'Have you put him on oxygen?' Gina asked, getting up. She didn't say anything when Rosie shook her head. She would run through the emergency procedures again with her later, after they had dealt with this crisis. Hurrying into the ward, she picked up the oxygen mask and swiftly fitted it over the patient's nose and mouth. 'Just try to breathe normally, Mr Jackson. That's it, nice and steady now. Good. You're doing great.'

She checked the monitor, noting that his pulse rate was much faster than it should have been and that his blood pressure was too low. Philip Jackson was forty-four years old and had been admitted via ED after complaining of being short of breath. His symptoms had disappeared since he had been on the unit and Miles Humphreys had concluded that the man had suffered nothing more serious than a panic attack. Miles had overruled her suggestion that Philip should remain there overnight for monitoring and had discharged him. Philip had actually been waiting for his wife to collect him when this had happened.

Gina bit back a sigh as she turned to Rosie. Miles wasn't going to be happy about being proved wrong. 'Can you ask the switchboard to page Dr Humphreys, please?'

She picked up the patient's notes as Rosie hurried away. The best way of dealing with Miles, she had found, was to be totally clued up about every aspect of a case. There was nothing of any significance in the notes that ED had made so she delved further into the file, frowning when she discovered that Philip Jackson had undergone surgery to repair a hernia three months earlier. It hadn't been included in the patient's recent history, but could it have a bearing on his present condition?

Miles arrived a few minutes later. Gina's heart sank when she saw him striding down the ward because she knew he was going to give her a hard time. Why wouldn't he just accept that she didn't want to go out with him? You couldn't *make* someone want to be with you, as she knew from experience. Unbidden her gaze went to Marco and she felt heat flow through her when she discovered that he was watching her. She hurriedly turned away, forcing herself to concentrate as Miles demanded to know what had happened.

'Mr Jackson has had difficulty breathing again.' She kept her gaze on the patient but she could feel Marco's eyes boring into her back. Had he remembered who she was? she wondered sickly. It was obvious that his memory was starting to return, so it could happen any time. What was she going to say if he asked her about her life? Could she simply ignore Lily's existence, pretend that she didn't have a daughter?

'I asked you a question, Sister. If it isn't too much to expect then I would like an answer.'

The sarcasm in Miles's voice cut through her musings and Gina jumped. 'I'm sorry, what did you say?'

Miles's expression darkened. 'I asked if any of the staff were present when the patient started to complain of shortness of breath.'

'No,' she replied truthfully. 'Rosie came to fetch me when the monitor started beeping.'

'I see. It appears that things are getting rather slack around here. If you'd been keeping a closer eye on your patients, Sister Lee, this might not have happened.'

Gina forbore to say anything. She knew that Miles would love it if she argued with him. The fact that he had discharged Philip Jackson didn't matter, it seemed. She waited silently while Miles examined him. Although Philip was responding to the oxygen, his blood pressure was still low. He also complained of having a pain in his chest which was worse every time he breathed.

'Keep him on oxygen for now and we'll see how he goes,' Miles instructed after he'd finished. 'I'm still not convinced it isn't another panic attack.'

'According to his notes, Mr Jackson had surgery to repair a hernia almost three months ago,' Gina pointed out levelly. 'Could that have any bearing on what's been happening recently?'

'Certainly not.' Miles's tone was scathing. 'If there was a problem following surgery, it would have shown up before now. I suggest you stick to nursing the patients, Sister, and leave the diagnoses to those of us who are qualified to make them.'

Gina's face flamed. It was galling to be spoken to that way. The visitors at the next bed had obviously heard what Miles had said because she could see the sympathy on their faces. However, before she could say anything another voice cut in.

'Sister has raised a valid point. It is an established fact that a pulmonary embolism can occur up to three months following surgery.'

Gina swung round, her eyes widening when she saw the grim expression on Marco's face. He wasn't looking at her, however; he was staring at Miles. His deeply accented tones were icy as he continued.

'I suggest you send the patient for a scan to rule out that possibility.'

A rush of heat ran up Miles's neck. 'I assure you that there is no need for you to get involved, Mr...um...' Miles stopped, obviously at a disadvantage because he didn't know Marco's name.

'Andretti. *Dr* Andretti,' Gina told him, placing

just enough emphasis on Marco's title that Miles couldn't fail to notice it. 'Dr Andretti is an expert on trauma care,' she added sweetly.

'Oh, I see.' If anything, Miles went even redder. 'Thank you, Dr Andretti. Rest assured that I shall bear your advice in mind,' he blustered.

Marco's expression didn't soften. 'You would be better off sending the patient to Radiology rather than waste time thinking about it. If it is a pulmonary embolism then time is of the essence.'

'I…ahem….yes, of course.' Miles hurriedly scribbled an instruction to that effect and thrust it into Gina's hands. 'See that Mr Jackson is sent for a scan immediately, Sister.'

'Of course,' Gina murmured as Miles hurried away. She told Philip Jackson that she would arrange for a porter to take him and moved away from the bed, pausing as she drew level with Marco. She wasn't sure why he had stood up for her, but she had to admit that it felt good to know that he had. She forced that foolish thought aside as she smiled politely at him. 'Thank you, Dr Andretti. I appreciated your help just now.'

'Prego!' He shrugged, drawing her attention to the solid width of his shoulders beneath the thin hospital gown. Although there wasn't an ounce of spare flesh on him, he had a leanly muscular physique that looked impressive in or out of clothes.

The thought was more than she could deal with and she started to move away, only to stop when he caught hold of her hand. Gina could feel the light pressure of his fingers on her skin and a wave of longing suddenly shot through her. It had been three years since she had felt his touch, three years since any man had touched her, because she'd not had another relationship since. Maybe that explained why it felt as though there was fire, not blood, running through her veins.

'I was happy to help...Gina.' His gaze held hers fast and she felt her heart rate increase when she saw the question in his eyes. In that second she knew that he had recognised her and panic rose up inside her.

'Look, Marco, this really isn't the time or the

place to discuss what happened between us,' she said urgently.

'No? Then when would be a good time?'

His tone was even so it was impossible to guess what he was thinking. Gina struggled to regain her control. She still hadn't made up her mind if she intended to tell him about Lily. When she had first found out that she was pregnant, she had decided to contact him. After all, he'd had a right to know that he was to be a father, although she'd planned to make it clear that she didn't expect anything from him. However, when she had failed to contact him by phone and the letter she had sent to his home had been returned, unopened, she had changed her mind.

Marco had made it abundantly clear that he wasn't interested in anything she had to tell him. To her mind, he had forfeited any rights he'd had and she wouldn't contact him again. However, that had been before he had reappeared in her life. Even though she loathed the idea, it made a difference. It was hard to know what to do, although one thing was certain: until she had made up her mind, she needed to stay calm.

'I don't know. The last thing I want is people talking, so maybe it would be better if we left things as they are until you're discharged.' She gave a sharp little laugh, hearing the strain it held and praying that Marco couldn't hear it. 'That's assuming we have anything to talk about. After all, it's not as though we parted the best of friends.'

CHAPTER FOUR

1 a.m. 12 December

MARCO couldn't sleep. It wasn't just the fact that he wasn't used to being surrounded by so many people that had kept him awake, but what Gina had said: *It's not as though we parted the best of friends.*

It didn't take a genius to work out that they must have had a relationship, but what sort exactly? The obvious answer was that they'd had an affair, but although there were gaps in his memory, he remembered enough to know that he didn't normally indulge in affairs. The thought of moving from one woman to the next purely for sexual gratification was anathema to him, but if that were the case, it meant that Gina must have played a very different role in his life.

He closed his eyes, wishing he could recall

what had gone on between them. Oh, he could remember all sorts of things now: where he had worked for the past few years—six months in Australia followed by two years in the USA. He also remembered why he had come to England— he had been head-hunted by one of London's top teaching hospitals. He should have been attending an interview for the post that very day, in fact. He would have to contact them and explain why he wasn't able to make it, although that didn't seem nearly as important as this. Why couldn't he remember what Gina had meant to him? All he knew was what she had told him, that their parting had been less than amicable. Hell!

Marco swore softly as he tossed back the bedclothes. Thankfully, his headache had gone and apart from the swelling above his right ear, there were few physical mementoes of the accident. If he could only fill in these gaps in his memory, he would be fine and definitely well enough to leave here. Quite frankly he'd had enough of being a patient!

His mouth compressed as he made his way

down the ward. He knew the two nurses had gone for their break because he had seen them leave. It meant that Gina was on her own, so it would be the ideal time to talk to her. He frowned as he stopped outside the office because he still didn't understand why she had been so reluctant to admit that she knew him. Obviously something serious must have happened between them in the past and he wouldn't rest until he found out what it was.

The thought spurred him on. He didn't bother knocking before he opened the door. Gina was sitting at the desk and he saw the surprise on her face when she glanced up.

'You were quick,' she began then trailed off when she saw him.

Marco saw the colour drain from her face and the fact that he had no idea what he had done to cause her to react that way angered him. His tone was harsher than he had intended it to be. 'I need to know what you meant when you said that we hadn't parted the best of friends.'

'And as I also said, this isn't the time or the

place to discuss it.' She stood up abruptly. 'Now, if you wouldn't mind returning to your bed, I have work to do.'

She took a couple of steps towards him, obviously intending to usher him from the room, but he stood his ground. Drawing himself up to his full six feet he stared haughtily down at her. 'I am not going anywhere until you explain what is going on. It's obvious from what you said that we have met before, so why did you choose not say anything sooner?'

She turned away, taking her time as she sat down. Marco could tell that she was struggling to gather her composure and was more perplexed than ever. Even if they'd had an affair, this was the twenty-first century and most young women would take it in their stride. So what was she so afraid of?

'I thought it best if I didn't say anything.'

Her voice was so low that he wondered if he had misheard her and frowned. 'Best? How? I don't understand.'

'Because…well, because they always say that

it's better if people remember things for themselves.' She took a quick breath and hurried on. 'If I'd told you everything I know about you then you'd never be sure if you'd remembered the details yourself or if I'd planted them in your mind, would you?'

It made sense, so much sense that Marco hesitated. It could very well explain why she had been so reluctant to acknowledge him and yet he had a gut feeling that there was more to it than that. A lot more, too.

'I see. So it was purely a desire to help me that kept you quiet,' he said smoothly.

'I… Yes, that's right.' A little colour touched her cheeks as she reached for her pen. 'I'm glad you understand that it was in your best interests that I said nothing, Dr Andretti.'

'And how about your interests, Gina? Was it in your best interests that you remain silent, I wonder?'

He knew he'd scored a hit when he saw her face pale but, oddly, it didn't give him any pleasure. To know that something must have happened in the past to make her so afraid of him was very hard to take. His tone was gentler when he continued, less confrontational. 'Look, Gina, I don't want to cause trouble. Not for you or for me. I just want to fill in as many of the blanks as possible.'

He shrugged, aware that it wasn't usual for him to admit to any feelings of weakness. Normally he preferred to keep his emotions under wraps but he needed to draw her out, if he could. 'I cannot begin to explain how terrifying it is not to be able to recall what has happened in your life. Even though I now remember quite a lot, there are many questions that still need answering.'

'What sort of questions?' she asked, and he frowned when he heard the tremor in her voice. It was obvious that she was under a great deal of strain and he hated to think that he was adding to the pressure on her, but he needed to find out all he could about this situation.

'I don't know!' he declared in sudden frustration. 'When you forget so much about your life, everything becomes a question. What do I enjoy doing when I'm not working, for instance? Where did I go for my last holiday? I can't answer either of those things!' He ran his hands through his hair, wishing he could physically force the memories to surface, and winced when his fingers encountered the tender spot above his ear.

'Sit down.' Gina was around the desk in a trice. She steered him towards a chair then went to the filing cabinet and switched on the kettle sitting on the top. 'I'll make you a cup of coffee. It's only instant, I'm afraid. Sorry. I know you dislike it but it's all we have.'

'That is exactly what I mean.' Marco sighed when she glanced round. 'I didn't know that I dislike instant coffee because I didn't remember.'

The ghost of a smile touched her mouth. 'Maybe I shouldn't have said anything then you wouldn't have been disappointed.'

Marco laughed. 'Ignorance is bliss—isn't that a saying you have in this country?'

'Yes, it is.' Her smile faded abruptly as she picked up the jar of coffee. 'Sometimes it's better to live in ignorance.'

Marco had no idea what to say to that. He knew

instinctively that she wasn't referring to his loss of memory and it puzzled him. What did she know that she didn't want anyone to find out?

His breath caught as he watched her pour boiling water into the mugs because he realised that he needed to amend that question. What did Gina know that she didn't want *him* finding out?

Gina placed the cups on the desk and sat down. She could feel herself trembling and took a deep breath. At some point during the past few minutes she had reached a decision. She wasn't going to tell Marco about Lily. Maybe she would regret it later but she would worry about it then. Right now, it seemed more important that she keep her daughter's existence a secret from him.

At the moment Lily was a happy and well-adjusted little girl. Gina had taken great care to ensure that the child enjoyed a stable home life. One of the reasons why she had ruled out having another relationship was because of the effect it could have on Lily. She had seen it happen to friends' children. New partners arrived on the scene and the family's dynamics had to alter accordingly. She didn't want that for Lily, didn't want her daughter to grow up surrounded by people who came and went in her life. She wanted Lily to have security.

If she told Marco about Lily, there was no knowing what he would do. Maybe he would be indifferent to the fact that he had a daughter but, more worryingly, he might want to play a role in the child's life, at least for a while. She couldn't bear to think that Lily might grow attached to him only to be let down at some point in the future. As she knew to her cost Marco could very easily change his mind.

Thoughts rushed through her head until she felt dizzy. She took a sip of her coffee, hoping it would steady her. If she was to stop Marco learning about Lily's existence then she would need to be extremely careful about what she said.

'How did we meet?'

She looked up when he spoke, feeling her heart jerk when she saw the way he was watching her so intently. He had always been very astute and she mustn't make the mistake of underestimating him. Although she hated to talk about the past, she knew it would be better to tell him the truth—as far as she could.

'I flew over to Florence to collect a patient you'd been treating,' she answered, pleased to hear that her voice held no trace of the nervousness she felt.

'I see.' He frowned. 'Obviously, you weren't working here at the time.'

'I worked for a company that repatriates clients to the UK when they're taken ill abroad.' She shrugged. 'The gentleman I was due to collect had suffered a stroke. It was supposed to be quite straightforward. I'd collect him from the hospital and accompany him back to England. Unfortunately, he suffered a second stroke shortly before I arrived and you decided that he wasn't fit to fly.'

'So what happened then? Did you return to England?'

Gina heard the curiosity in his voice and realised there was no point prevaricating. 'No. The patient's family asked if I would stay while he was in hospital. He was on his own and they felt it would help if he had someone with him.' She shrugged. 'The family offered to pay my salary and the firm I worked for agreed to let me take some leave, so I said yes.'

'For how long?' Marco demanded.

'Six weeks.'

His brows rose. 'That seems an excessive amount of time to me. Surely your patient was fit to travel before then?'

This was the difficult bit, the part she didn't want to explain. 'Sadly, the patient died a week later.'

'But you didn't go home?'

She shook her head.

'Why not?'

'I'd never visited Florence before and it seemed like the perfect opportunity to see something of the city and surrounding area.'

'So you stayed to do some sightseeing?' His tone was flat and she couldn't blame it for the shiver that passed through her. It took every scrap of composure she could muster to answer.

'Yes.' She stood up, making a great show of checking her watch. 'I'm sorry but I really do need to get on.'

'Of course.' He stood up as well, looking so big and male as he towered over that her heart beat all the harder. 'Will you just answer me one final question, Gina?'

'If I can.'

'Did you also stay on in Florence because of me?'

Gina bit her lip. She could lie, of course, but she knew him well enough to guess that he would see through it. Tipping back her head, she looked him in the eyes. 'Yes, I did. Now, if that's all...'

She walked around the desk, steeling herself as she passed him. How she ached to touch him, to lay her hand on his arm and tell him the rest, that she had stayed because she had fallen in love with him, had thought he had loved her too, but what was the point? No doubt Marco would re-member it all in time, remember those few glorious weeks they'd had before he had realised that he had no longer wanted her, although his memory of what had happened must be very different from hers. Tears pricked her eyes and she turned away. She refused to let him see her cry, refused to let him take away her dignity as well as everything else!

'I am sorry, Gina, so very sorry that I can't remember.'

The regret in his voice was almost too much. Somehow she made it out of the door but it was hard to hold onto her composure. When Julie came back from her break, she told her she was going to the canteen and hurriedly departed. And as the lift swept her up to the top floor, the tears that she had held at bay trickled down her cheeks.

She had loved Marco so much! Loved him with her heart, her soul and every scrap of her being, but it hadn't been enough. Not for him. He had taken her love and tossed it back in her face and there was no way that she would risk that happening again.

Gina took a deep breath as the lift came to a

halt. Whatever she and Marco had had was over. What she needed to focus on now was Lily—the one good thing to have come out of the whole terrible experience. So long as Lily was safe and happy, nothing else mattered.

If he had hoped that talking to Gina would set his mind at rest, Marco was disappointed. He spent the night thinking about what he had learned or, more importantly, what he hadn't. He sensed that Gina was keeping something from him and had no idea how he could find out what it was. Maybe he should wait until his memory returned of its own accord and go from there?

He sighed. He had no idea how long it would be before he could remember everything that had happened and he wasn't sure if he could wait. It was obvious that Gina wasn't going to tell him anything else, so if he was to find out what she was keeping from him then he would have to start digging for the information himself. And to do that, he needed to get out of here. When

Steven Pierce arrived shortly after eight a.m. Marco could barely contain his impatience.

'Good morning, Dr Andretti. How are you feeling today?' Steven enquired as he lifted Marco's chart off the end of the bed. The night staff had gone off duty by then and there was another nurse with him who introduced herself as Sister Thomas. Marco found himself wishing that it was Gina standing there, Gina with her soothing voice, her gentle manner, her beautiful smile. The world always seemed a much nicer place when Gina was around.

The thought slid into his head and he knew that it had occurred to him before. There was a familiarity about it that resonated deep inside him. Marco took a quick breath, feeling little waves of panic rippling along his veins. Gina had meant something to him in the past, something more than he would have expected if they'd had a casual affair. And the fact that any woman could have had this effect on him after Francesca stunned him.

'Dr Andretti?'

'Scusi.' Marco hurriedly marshalled his thoughts when he realised that Steven was waiting for him to answer. 'I am feeling a lot better this morning, thank you.'

'Good. That's what we like to hear, isn't it, Sister?'

'Indeed, Doctor.'

Marco tried not to wince when the woman spoke. She had a particularly irritating voice, rather nasal and high-pitched, completely different from Gina's low, sweet tones… He stamped down hard on that thought, forcing himself to concentrate as Steven asked him a series of questions aimed, Marco suspected, at checking how much of his memory had returned.

'That's excellent,' the registrar concluded. 'You obviously recall a lot more today than you did yesterday. Most people suffering from retrograde amnesia find that the gap in their memory continues to shrink over a period of time. I'm hoping that is what will happen with you.'

'Do you have any idea how long it will be before I remember everything?' Marco demanded.

Maybe he would feel easier if he knew that in a week's time, say, he would remember all about him and Gina. What was so frustrating was the fact that he had no idea when the details of their relationship would come back to him.

'Sadly, that's a question I can't answer. It could be hours or it could be months.' Steven's tone was sombre. 'To be perfectly frank, Dr Andretti, your memory might never come back completely. It's one of the hardest things anyone who has suffered from amnesia has to live with, the feeling that there may be something he or she can't remember. All I can advise you to do is to take it one step at a time and see what happens.'

Marco knew that it was good advice, advice he, himself, would have given a patient. However, it was very different being on the receiving end. 'Surely there is something you can do to speed up the process!'

'I'm afraid not.' Steven looked a little taken aback by his vehemence. 'Rest and relaxation are what will help most at the moment. That's why I've arranged for you to be transferred to a private room. You should find it more peaceful there.'

'No.' Marco shook his head. 'I have no intention of remaining here. I feel perfectly fine, quite well enough to leave.'

'Oh, I really don't think that is a good idea,' Steven began, but Marco held up his hand.

'I have made my decision. Physically, I am fit enough to leave, do you agree?'

'Well, yes,' Steven conceded.

'*Bene.* So the only problem I have is my inability to remember everything that has happened in the past and as you have just told me, Dr Pierce, there is no knowing how long it will be before that issue resolves itself.' He shrugged. 'I cannot remain here indefinitely.'

'I appreciate that, Dr Andretti. However, a couple more days could make a huge difference,' Steven insisted. 'With rest and relaxation, maybe some counselling, we could achieve a real breakthrough.'

'I can rest at my hotel,' Marco assured him, knowing the younger man had his best interests at heart. That thought reminded him of what Gina had said and he knew that no matter what else happened, he had to get to the bottom of this mystery. If he and Gina had been more than simply lovers, he needed to know!

The thought sent a rush of heat coursing through him and he cleared his throat, stunned by the speed of his response. Although Gina was a beautiful woman, he had met other equally beautiful women over the past few years and had never reacted this strongly. What was it about her that seemed to touch him on so many levels? he wondered. He had no idea but he couldn't deny that she affected him deeply.

'I appreciate your concern, Dr Pierce, but I assure you that I know what I'm doing,' he said, forcing himself to focus on the issue at hand. 'I shall leave this morning and go to my hotel.'

'Do you remember where you're staying?' Steven put in quickly.

Marco named the hotel and smiled wryly. 'I stay there whenever I'm in London, as I recall.'

'I see.' Steven looked resigned. 'Obviously, I

can't keep you here against your will, but I do hope you'll be sensible, Dr Andretti. If you experience any problems, please get in touch with us immediately.'

'I shall.' Marco smiled as he held out his hand. 'Thank you for everything. You have been extremely kind.'

'Just doing my job,' Steven assured him, shaking hands.

Marco didn't waste a single moment after the other man left. He drew the curtains around the bed and got dressed. His clothes looked decidedly worse for wear but as he didn't have anything else, he put them on. He had no idea what had happened to his luggage. It was probably still in the back of the hire car, but that was the least of his worries. How long would it be before he remembered what had happened between him and Gina? A day? A week? A month? A year?

He shook his head. He couldn't wait that long. He had to persuade her to tell him the truth, but it wasn't going to be easy. All he could do was try to gain her trust—if he could. Something warned him that getting Gina to trust him was going to be an uphill struggle.

CHAPTER FIVE

12 December

GINA was dreading going into work that night in case Marco was still there. Although he should have been transferred by now, it depended on whether a bed had been found for him. It was a relief when she discovered that the end bay was occupied by another patient. At least she wouldn't have to field any more awkward questions that night, although she wasn't foolish enough to think it would be the end of the matter. Marco obviously suspected something was wrong and she knew him well enough to know that he wouldn't simply give up.

Panic assailed her at the thought of the harm it could cause if he found out about Lily. If only she could predict how he would react, it would be so much easier, but that was something she couldn't do. She had no idea if he would be thrilled or furious to learn he had a daughter, and no idea at all how he would feel about it in the long term. As she knew from experience, Marco could blow hot one minute and cold the next, and there was no way that Lily was going to be subjected to his mood swings.

Gina's heart was heavy as she set to work. It wasn't in her nature to be deceitful, but she had to do what she believed was best for Lily. Rosie was working again that night so they made a start on the obs. Julie was supposed to be on duty as well but there was no sign of her. Gina knew they wouldn't be able to manage with a member of staff short and went into the office to phone the nursing manager to see if she could provide cover. She had just picked up the phone when Julie came rushing in.

'Sorry! My car broke down and I had to leave it in the street and walk the rest of the way.' Julie looked worried as she unravelled her scarf. 'I hope it won't cost a fortune to get it fixed.

With Christmas just around the corner, money's really tight.'

'Fingers crossed it will be something minor,' Gina said sympathetically. Julie had three teenage children and Gina knew how hard she and her husband worked to pay all the bills.

'Fingers *and* toes,' Julie agreed, grimacing. 'Right, so what needs doing first? Obs?'

'Please. It's not quite as hectic as last night but we're still pretty full. Go and put your coat away and then we'll finish the obs. Bearing in mind that it's Friday, I'm sure business will pick up soon.'

'Bound to,' Julie replied cheerfully. 'By the way, is that dishy Italian doctor still with us? It would be nice to have a stunner like him to look at instead of the usual Friday night drunks.'

Gina dredged up a smile. 'You're out of luck, I'm afraid. There's another patient in the end bay so I assume he's been moved to Neurology.'

'Pity. I could have done with a pick-me-up after the evening I've had.'

Julie laughed as she hurried away. Gina sighed

as she went to check on Rosie. She didn't want to keep thinking about Marco but it was impossible not to do so. It was the uncertainty that was worst of all, the fact that she had no idea what he would do next. Would he seek her out and try to get more information out of her about their past?

The thought made her stomach churn. Every time she spoke to him, she ran the risk of saying something revealing, and it was worrying to know how easily she could trip up. Quite frankly, it would suit her fine if she never had to see Marco Andretti again!

Marco spent the day resting in his hotel room. Despite his claims, he felt far weaker than he had expected when he had left the hospital. It was a relief when the porter showed him to his room.

He tipped the man and asked him to send up a pot of coffee. Although there were coffee-making facilities in the room, he couldn't face another cup of instant brew. Gina was right—he did hate it—and the fact that she remembered such a minor detail seemed to highlight this problem he had. They must have been very close if she knew his likes and dislikes, so why couldn't he remember what had gone on between them?

He sighed wearily because there was no answer to that question. Stripping off his clothes, he went into the bathroom and took a shower. Wrapping himself in one of the thick towelling robes hanging behind the door, he went back to the bedroom and phoned housekeeping. By the time the waiter arrived with his coffee, he had arranged for his suit to be dry cleaned and half a dozen white shirts and assorted underwear to be delivered to his room. At least he would have some clean clothes to wear while he waited for his suitcase to turn up, he thought as he poured himself a cup of the fragrant brew, automatically inhaling the aroma of freshly ground beans...

Gina used to laugh at him whenever he did that, he thought suddenly. She used to tease him about being addicted to the smell of coffee. He could picture them now sitting in their favourite café overlooking the River Arno. Her slate-grey eyes were dancing with amusement, her cheeks pink from the heat in the café. It was winter and everyone was bundled up in scarves and hats. Gina didn't have a scarf so he had given her his; the dark grey mohair was the perfect foil for her blonde hair. She looked so beautiful as she sat there laughing at him that he couldn't help himself. He simply leaned across the table and kissed her.

Marco shuddered as the image melted away. The memory had been so clear that he could feel his lips tingling from the contact with hers. Gina had told him that it had been three years since they had met, yet it felt as though it was mere seconds since he had kissed her, felt the warm urgency of her mouth as she had kissed him back.

He stood up abruptly, not proof against how it made him feel to discover that Gina had felt something for him, too. At the back of his mind he had been hoping they had merely had a fling, out of character for him, granted, but perfectly acceptable between two consenting adults. However, that theory had been shot right out of the water. He wouldn't have felt this intensely when he had kissed her if she'd been just someone he had slept

with; she wouldn't have responded so passion-
ately if he had been a one-night stand.

Marco went to the window and stared out.
There was no point trying to pretend that their
relationship had been no more than a fleeting affair. It had been much more than that.

'Her blood alcohol reading is 450 milligrams per
100 millilitres. According to her friends, she only
had a couple of glasses of wine, too.' The ED
nurse rolled his eyes. 'Call me a cynic but somehow I don't think that's true, do you?'

'Not from the look of it.' Gina looked sadly
down at the girl lying on the bed. Katie Morris
was seventeen years old and a student at sixth-
form college. She had been out celebrating the
end of term with a group of friends but had
carried the celebrations too far. She had been
brought into ED after collapsing in the street and
subsequently been moved to AAU. She would
need careful monitoring with that level of alcohol in her system.

'Thanks, Terry, we'll take it from here. Have

her parents been informed, do you know?' Gina asked.

'A message was left on their answering-machine requesting that they contact the hospital,' Terry informed her. 'Not heard anything yet, though.'

'Hopefully, they'll get in touch soon,' Gina replied, deftly attaching the girl to one of their monitors. She did Katie's obs, noting down her BP, sats and pulse rate on the chart. The teenager was still unconscious and likely to remain that way after the amount of alcohol she had consumed. Sadly, far too many youngsters failed to understand that alcohol taken in such quantities caused acute poisoning and could prove fatal.

Gina made sure the girl was comfortable. She had just finished when Julie came to tell her there was a phone call for her. She hurried into the office and picked up the receiver. 'Sister Lee speaking. How may I help you?'

'Gina, it's Marco.'

The shock of hearing his voice stunned her into silence. There was a brief pause before he continued and she couldn't fail to hear the impatience in his voice. 'Did you hear what I said? It's Marco.'

'I...um...I thought you were on the neurology unit.' It took every scrap of willpower to reply calmly when her heart was racing. Why was he phoning her? What did he want? Surely he hadn't found out about Lily, had he? The questions tumbled around inside her head, so that she missed what he said and had to ask him to repeat it.

'I said that I discharged myself this morning,' he repeated, his deep voice grating. 'There was no point in my staying in hospital. If I am to recover my memory then I need to find out all I can. That is why I have to talk to you.'

'I'm sorry but I can't talk now,' she said, hurriedly. 'I'm far too busy.'

'I appreciate that, which is why I am phoning to set up a time and a place when we can meet.'

Gina's heart sank. The last thing she wanted was to meet him. 'I really can't see the point. I've told you everything I can, Dr Andretti.'

'Have you indeed?' His tone was silky yet there was no mistaking the scepticism it held.

'Yes,' she retorted. 'Now, I'm very sorry but I really don't have the time right now...'

'I have remembered, Gina.'

Gina paused uncertainly. 'Remembered?'

'*Si.* Oh, I can't recall everything that happened between us but I know that we were close at one point.' His voice dropped and she shivered when she felt the richly accented tones stroking along her nerves. 'We were lovers, weren't we?'

'I...' She had to stop and swallow to unlock the knot in her throat. She was tempted to deny the allegation but what was the point if Marco had remembered? 'Yes, we were.'

'I thought so. I remembered us being in a café overlooking the River Arno. It was a cold day and you were wearing my scarf. *Si?*'

Heat flowed through her as she instantly recalled the occasion. Marco had managed to wangle some time off work and they had spent the afternoon strolling through the city. It had been bitterly cold, the river shimmering steel-grey under a wintry sky, but it hadn't mattered. Just being with Marco, feeling his hand clasped around hers as they had strolled along the busy streets, had filled her with warmth and happiness. And when they had stopped for coffee and he had leaned across the table and kissed her, she had known her life would never be the same again. That was the moment when she had realised that she was in love with him, the moment when it had felt that all her dreams were about to come true.

Pain seared through her. It was all she could do not to cry out but she couldn't afford to let him know how much he had hurt her. If she could pass off their relationship as little more than a brief affair then he would stop digging for information and Lily would be safe. 'I can't say that I remember it in particular, but I'm sure it happened if you say it did.'

'Of course.' His tone was as unrevealing as hers had been so Gina couldn't explain why she knew that he was disappointed by her answer. Surely he hadn't wanted her to remember that kiss, had he?

The thought was both poignant and foolish.

She brushed it aside, knowing how stupid it was. Marco had been perfectly clear when he had broken up with her, so what was the point of harking back to the past?

'I'm pleased that your memory is coming back, but I really cannot see what I can do to help. Yes, we were lovers at one point but I haven't seen you since we split up. I have no knowledge whatsoever of what's happened in your life in the past three years.'

'The past three years are probably what I remember best,' he informed her. 'I remember where I worked as well as the people I worked with—all the details like that.'

'Then you're obviously on the way to making a full recovery.' Gina knew that she had to wind up the conversation. The more she said, the greater the risk that something might slip out. 'All I can do is wish you well. I hope that everything works out for you, Dr Andretti.'

'Marco.'

'Pardon?'

'My name is Marco. Bearing in mind that we

have been so intimate with each other, I find it rather ridiculous that you insist on being so formal.'

There was a teasing note in his voice that immediately stirred her senses. Although Marco gave the appearance of being a very serious person, he had a wicked sense of humour and had loved to tease her.

The thought sent another little stab of pain through her heart but she ignored it. She refused to look back, refused to go down the path of 'what if'. Marco hadn't wanted her three years ago and he didn't want her now. 'Marco,' she echoed, allowing a touch of weariness to creep into her voice.

'*Bene.* Now we are making progress. Let us hope that we can continue to do so, Gina.'

'I have no idea what you mean by that. I have just explained that I can't tell you anything else that might help. We had an affair. It lasted six weeks and when it was over I returned to England. That's it. There's nothing to add.'

'Are you sure?' His tone was calm. There was

no hint of threat in it yet all of a sudden she felt scared, really scared.

'Of course I am! Now I'm sorry but I have to go. Goodbye, Dr.....Marco. I hope everything works out for you.'

She dropped the phone back onto its rest. It was obvious that Marco suspected something, but what? She wished she knew because maybe then she would have known how to deal with the situation. Knowing Marco, he wouldn't be content to leave things as they were. He would seek her out again, press her for more information, and each time he did so the risk of him finding out about Lily would intensify.

She needed to get away, she decided. Go someplace where he couldn't find her and that way Lily would be safe. However, it wasn't that easy to up and leave. She would need to find somewhere to live, another job so she could support them, and then there was the problem of childcare. Lily was happy with the childminder Gina had found to look after her while she was at work. Not all childminders were prepared to care for children whose parents worked shifts and she had been lucky to find Amy. Running away would entail as many problems as staying and facing Marco, it seemed.

All of a sudden Gina felt torn in two. Lily could be badly hurt if she stayed, yet she could be equally hurt if she was taken away from everything and everyone she knew.

CHAPTER SIX

GINA had the following four days off so once she finished work she collected Lily and took her home to the small basement flat they shared. With its tiny living room and minuscule kitchen, it wasn't exactly luxurious living, but she had done her best to brighten up the place by hanging lots of colourful prints on the walls.

She had also partitioned off a corner of the bedroom so the little girl had her own space complete with a child-sized bed. They were comfortable enough, although she was very aware that they would have to move when Lily grew bigger. Still, that was something to worry about in the future. At the present time she had other matters on her mind.

She gave Lily a drink then helped her build a tower out of some wooden blocks. Lily had a nap after her lunch and usually Gina tried to snatch an hour's sleep then. By the time Lily was tucked up, Gina's eyelids were drooping so she lay down on the couch. However, the minute she closed her eyes it all came rushing back: Marco and his questions and what she had—and hadn't—told him. Should she have told him the truth? Had she been right to withhold such an important piece of information from him? Was it fair to Lily not to tell her that Marco was her father?

By the time Lily woke up, Gina felt dreadful. The combination of tiredness and guilt had left her feeling wrung out. If this was how she felt after just a couple of days of covering up her secret, how much worse would she feel in a week or so's time? Surely telling Marco the truth couldn't be any worse than this?

Just for a second she wavered before her resolve stiffened. This had nothing to do with how *she* felt and everything to do with how it could affect Lily. No matter how hard it was, it would be a mistake to tell Marco about his daughter.

Marco spent the following week wondering what to do. His memory was returning rapidly and he now had a fairly comprehensive picture of what his life had been like. However, the one memory he yearned to recall continued to elude him.

Apart from a few tantalising flashes, his relationship with Gina was still a blank and the worst thing was knowing it could remain that way if she refused to tell him what had really happened. It was obvious that she was scared of him and he had no idea why. Maybe he couldn't remember everything he'd ever done, but he knew enough to be sure that he would never harm a woman physically.

He sighed. Rationally, he knew that he should stop worrying about Gina. So they'd had an affair and it had ended badly—so what? He should accept it and move on, but it was proving impossible to do so. There was just something about her that drew him, something that made him unable to dismiss her from his thoughts. He needed to uncover the truth about their relationship. Although he had shied away from the idea of falling in love again after Francesca had died, he only had to recall how he had kissed Gina in that café to know that he had felt something for her.

Had he been in love with her? Was he even capable of loving a woman again?

He couldn't answer either of those questions but in his heart he knew that the rest of his life could depend on what he did now and it scared him to realise that Gina could hold the key to his future.

Gina was on days when she went back into work. AAU was as busy as ever and the morning flew past; before she knew it, it was time for lunch. She decided to go to the canteen and headed for the lift. She was just about to step inside when she heard someone calling her and looked round to see Marco striding towards her.

Her heart sank. She really didn't want to talk to him, but what choice did she have? She couldn't afford to do anything that would arouse his suspicions even more. She pinned a polite smile to her lips as he came closer. 'This is a surprise. I didn't expect to see you here.'

'I have an appointment,' he replied evenly.

He waited for her to step into the lift, pressing

the button for the fifth floor once she had selected her destination, and Gina frowned. The fifth floor was home to the administration department and she couldn't help wondering what business he had up there. She was on the point of asking him when she thought better of it. It would be safer if she didn't show any interest in his affairs.

'Has it been a busy day?' he enquired as the lift carried them up.

'It always is.'

'It can't help that you're carrying a number of vacancies at the moment, though. That must put added pressure on the staff.'

Gina frowned, unsure where he had gleaned that information. 'It does. One of our registrars is off sick and won't be back for another month, and our consultant retired at the end of October. They did hire a replacement, but he pulled out. They've advertised the post again, but it could take a while to find someone suitable.'

'Good staff are difficult to find,' he agreed. He

glanced round when the lift came to a halt. 'Ah, my floor, I think. Enjoy your lunch.'

'Thank you,' Gina murmured. She put out her hand to stop the doors from closing as she peered after him, trying to see where he was going, but he rounded a corner and disappeared from sight. She sighed as she continued her journey. She should just be glad that he hadn't tried to cross-examine her. Maybe his interest in her was waning?

The thought should have been a comfort yet she couldn't help feeling deflated. She had expected Marco to give her a much harder time in his desire to uncover the past but it appeared he was no longer interested.

Had he already recalled what had happened? she wondered suddenly. And now he had remembered their affair and his reasons for ending it, there was no need to question her any more? So far as he was concerned that was the end of the matter.

Just for a second she experienced an overwhelming sense of guilt at not telling him about

Lily before she dismissed it. It was far better that Marco didn't know about their daughter. He could go back to Italy and get on with his life while she and Lily got on with theirs. There was no reason why they should see one another again.

CHAPTER SEVEN

February

IT HAD taken Marco far longer than he had expected to finalise the details. First there had been the necessary checks to ensure that he was fit to do the job. Then, once he'd overcome that hurdle, there had been the usual contractual delays. Now, however, as he stared up at the grey concrete façade of the hospital, he found himself wondering if he had been mad to make such a life-changing decision.

He *never* did things on a whim. He *always* weighed up the pros and cons beforehand, yet here he was, about to jump in at the deep end, and for what? To solve a mystery that might not even exist? To find answers to questions that might not need to be asked? Hell!

His mouth thinned as he pushed open the door.

He knew there would be a reception committee waiting to greet him on the fifth floor but strode straight past the lifts. He didn't want thanks for taking on the post of locum consultant in charge of AAU when there had been nothing altruistic about his decision. He had done it for one reason and one reason alone: he needed to know what had happened between him and Gina to make her so wary of him.

AAU was busy when he arrived. He paused in the doorway, feeling his heart jolt when he spotted Gina standing near the window. She was talking to an elderly female patient and didn't appear to have noticed him so he had time to take stock.

Marco felt his blood quicken as he studied the delicate line of her profile. Her skin was so fine that it appeared almost translucent in the pale morning light filtering through the glass, the rose-pink blush that tinted her cheeks making his fingers suddenly itch to touch it. Her skin would feel like the inside of a rose petal, he thought wonderingly, so soft and smooth, so warm and velvety.

A shudder ran through him and he took a deep breath, knowing that he couldn't afford to let his emotions run away with him. In the past few weeks he had found it increasingly hard to keep them under control. Maybe it was the fact that he still couldn't remember this affair he'd had with Gina that had upset his emotional balance— he didn't know. But where once he could have buried his feelings, now they seemed to lie just beneath the surface, ready to erupt at the least excuse.

She suddenly looked up and he stiffened when their eyes met. Just for a moment her expression was blank before he saw her lips part in a tiny gasp. This was the moment he had been antici- pating for weeks, yet all of a sudden he wasn't sure what to do. Should he go to her or let her come to him?

The decision was taken from him when some- one rudely elbowed him aside. Marco swung round, his annoyance fading when he saw the anxious face of the porter who was pushing a trolley bearing a small child into the ward.

'Sorry, mate, but this is an emergency,' the man muttered, hurrying past him. There was a nurse with him and she had to run to keep up as the porter propelled the trolley towards an empty bay.

'Chloe Daniels, aged seven. She arrested when we were halfway along the corridor,' the nurse explained. She squeezed the ambubag she had placed over the child's nose and mouth. 'Can someone give me a hand, please?'

Marco reacted instinctively. Crossing the room in a couple of strides, he bent over the child. 'Why was she admitted?' he demanded as he checked for a pulse.

'Suspected concussion. She fell off a garden wall and banged her head. Her mum didn't see it happen and wasn't sure if Chloe had passed out, so she's being kept in for monitoring.' The nurse looked uncertainly at him. 'I'm sorry but who are you exactly?'

'Dr Andretti,' Marco replied shortly, hoping she wasn't going to ask for proof of his identity. He should have collected his ID tag after meeting the reception committee, but as he had avoided that pleasure he had nothing to back up his claim...unless Gina would vouch for him.

He glanced round when she appeared, doing his best to behave like the professional he was. Never in the whole of his working life had he allowed his personal feelings to intrude on his work, yet they were in danger of doing so now. 'Sister Lee knows who I am,' he replied tersely, not appreciating the fact that he was behaving so out of character. 'I am sure she will vouch for me. Won't you, Sister?'

'Yes. I know Dr Andretti,' she replied in a tight little voice.

Marco shot her a quick glance before he returned his attention to the child but it was enough to tell him how shocked she was to see him. She looked as though the bottom had dropped out of her world and the thought touched an already raw nerve. Come what may, he *had* to get to the bottom of this mystery!

Gina could feel ripples of shock spreading through her body. She had no idea what Marco was doing there...

She gasped. There had been rumours flying around for weeks that someone had been appointed to the consultant's post, but the powers-that-be had neither confirmed nor denied them. Everyone had put it down to the fact that they hadn't wished to suffer any further embarrassment if the new appointee decided to pull out, but maybe there was another explanation. Maybe Marco had asked them to withhold the information for his own reasons?

The thought that those reasons might have something to do with her made her stomach churn with nerves but she fought to control them. Positioning herself beside the bed, she glanced at Marco. 'I'll start chest compressions.'

'*Si.*'

He stepped aside as she began pressing lightly on the little girl's chest. The method for resuscitating a child was the same as for an adult; the only difference was the amount of pressure needed. Too much force and ribs could be cracked so she took extra care, working in sync with the ED nurse who was maintaining the child's breathing.

'*Un momento.*'

Gina stopped as Marco bent over the child. He checked the pulse in her neck, his long fingers with their olive-toned skin looking dark against the little girl's flesh.

'*Bene!* We have a pulse. Put her on a monitor and let us see how she goes. Has she had a CT scan?'

'Yes, Dr Andretti.' The nurse produced a hand-held computer and showed him the results of the scan. 'Dr Humphreys checked it and said it was clear.'

Marco scrolled through the images. He frowned as he studied one particular frame. 'There is a hairline fracture on the right side of her head. It is difficult to see, but it is definitely there. See.'

He showed the screen to Gina, pointing out the area in question, but it still took her a moment to see what he was referring to. 'There does appear to be a very fine fracture,' she agreed finally.

'I want another scan. We need to see if there is a bleed in the area. That would explain why she arrested.' Marco was all business as he rapped out instructions. 'Can you get onto Theatre and inform them that I may need to operate? Where are her parents?'

'Her mum went outside to phone the grand-mother,' the ED nurse explained. 'She should be along any moment.'

'Good. I'll leave it to you to ensure the relevant forms are signed so the operation can go ahead if need be, Sister.'

'Of course, Dr Andretti.'

Gina didn't waste time querying how and why he had the right to set things in motion. The explanations would come later, although there didn't seem much to explain. Her heart sank as she went to the office and put through a call requesting a second scan. It appeared that Marco was indeed their new consultant and it didn't take a genius to work out why he had decided to take the post. The thought of what he might uncover made her knees go weak. She knew that if he found out about Lily it would be even worse now. He would be furious that she hadn't told him sooner, when she'd had the chance to do so.

The thought of facing his wrath on top of everything else was almost too much. Gina could barely concentrate as she contacted Theatre and informed them that Dr Andretti would probably require a slot shortly. Naturally, that triggered a whole host of questions as to who Dr Andretti was, where he had worked previously, and whether he seemed a bit more clued-up than their previous consultant had been.

Gina pleaded pressure of work to wriggle out of divulging anything more than the basics—that he was Italian and seemed extremely competent. However, she knew the questions would be coming thick and fast as everyone tried to find out all they could about their new boss and not just about his working methods either. His private life was bound to attract a great deal of interest, too.

What would *Marco* tell them? she wondered as she hung up. Would he mention her, admit that they'd had an affair?

She hoped not because it would make her situation even more precarious. All it would take was for some bright spark to do the maths, work out that Lily must be his daughter, and that would be it—her secret would be out. She groaned in dismay. Why in heaven's name had Marco decided to pursue this?

'Swab, please.'

Marco waited while the blood was swabbed away. So far the operation to relieve the pressure on little Chloe's brain had gone quite smoothly. He had made a burr hole through which the blood had been drained away. He was confident that the child would make a full recovery and nodded in satisfaction as he placed a dressing over the wound.

'*Bene.* Thank you, everyone. It is always good to work with a skilled team.'

A collective sigh of relief greeted that statement. As Marco exited Theatre a short time later, he heard the hum of conversation break out. No doubt they were discussing him, he thought as he headed for the changing room. It was always an uncertain time for staff when they met their new boss and in this case it must be doubly difficult for them. They didn't know him so they were bound to have concerns. Hopefully, he had convinced them that he knew what he was doing, although, realistically, it would take time for them to accept him. Maybe Gina would put in a good word for him, he mused as he switched on the shower, then realised how foolish it was to hope for that. From the expression on her face when she had seen him that morning, it was doubtful if she would have anything good to say about him!

It was an unsettling thought. Marco tried not to dwell on it as he changed back into his clothes. Gina was with a patient when he returned to the unit so he waited until she had finished and called her over. 'I need a word with Chloe's mother. Is there a room I can use?'

'Yes. It's through here.' Gina showed him into a small but comfortable sitting room, with twin sofas set either side of a coffee table.

Marco nodded. 'This is fine. Are both her parents here, do you know?'

'I'm not sure. Ruth—that's the nurse who accompanied her from ED—only mentioned her mother.'

'In that case, I would like you to stay while I speak to her.' He shrugged when Gina looked at him in surprise. 'She might feel more at ease with another woman present.'

'Oh. Well, yes, of course I'll stay. Do you want me to fetch her in now?'

'*Si.* Chloe will be leaving Recovery shortly. I am sure her mother will be anxious to be there when she returns.'

Marco smiled pleasantly but Gina didn't respond as she left the room. He sighed, wondering how he was going to approach the task of gaining her trust. It was going to be an uphill battle from the look of it but he intended to keep on until he wore down her defences and convinced her that he wasn't going to hurt her in any way.

He frowned when it struck him that he couldn't guarantee that she wouldn't get hurt. As he knew nothing about what lay behind her fear of him, he couldn't make such a promise. It worried him that he might end up doing something to cause her even more distress but what choice did he have?

If he gave up now, he might never find out this secret she was keeping from him. Although he had been passed as fit to work, there were still a few blank spots in his memory. The specialist he had seen had been pragmatic: he might remember everything eventually and he might not. Maybe he could live with the thought that he had forgotten the odd minor detail, but he couldn't live with not knowing about his relationship with Gina. It was far too important, even though he wasn't sure why.

Marco tried to put that thought aside when Gina appeared with Chloe's mother. 'Mrs Daniels, I'm Dr Andretti. I operated on your daughter.'

He shook hands then ushered her towards one of the sofas. Gina sat down as well, her expression betraying very little as she waited for him to speak, yet he sensed her inner turmoil. It made him feel guilty to know that he was the cause of it, too. He cleared his throat, refusing to allow himself to be sidetracked.

'First of all I want to say that the operation went very smoothly. I am confident that it has resolved the problem.'

'Thank heavens!' Donna Daniels seemed to crumple in her seat. Marco could see tears in her eyes and smiled sympathetically.

'I know it must have been a very worrying time for you, Mrs Daniels, but I am sure that Chloe will be fine. She will need a few days to get over the operation so she will be transferred to the children's ward once she leaves Recovery. She may have a headache for a few days but that will pass and I am not anticipating any long-term problems.'

'Thank you, Doctor. I can't tell you how relieved I am to hear that.' Donna sighed shakily. 'I still don't know how it happened. Chloe was playing in the garden while I got ready to take her to school. She was only on her own for a couple of minutes but when I went out, she was lying on the ground...'

She broke off and gulped, obviously distraught at the thought of her daughter coming to harm.

Marco watched as Gina leant over and squeezed her hand.

'It isn't your fault, Donna. You can't watch a child every minute of the day.'

'Maybe not but I should have realised she might try to climb up that wall at some point!'

'If it wasn't a wall then it would be something else.' Gina smiled, her slate-grey eyes filled with compassion, and Marco felt the strangest emotion rise up inside him. He was jealous, he realised in amazement. Jealous at the thought of her sparing all that emotion for someone else when he wanted it for himself.

The thought shocked him so that it was an effort to focus on the conversation. He had never experienced jealousy before, not even for Francesca, and the realisation was like a knife being thrust through his ribs. He had loved Francesca yet he had never felt this way about *her*!

'Children always manage to do the one thing you never expect. It's as though they have some kind of sixth-sense that makes them home in on danger. Why, only the other day I found my daughter perched on a chair, attempting to reach a vase that I'd put out of her way. Another second and she'd have got it *and* probably dropped it, too!'

The two women laughed but Marco didn't join in. He couldn't because he didn't have enough breath to spare. *Gina had a daughter?* Was it true? Or was it something she had made up to console the other woman?

He stared at her and saw the dawning horror on her face when she realised why he was looking at her. In that second he knew that he had uncovered her secret, found out what she had been keeping from him. What he didn't understand, though, was why she had been so determined to keep the child's existence from him.

He took a deep breath, his head reeling. He may have solved one mystery but now, it appeared, he needed to solve another.

CHAPTER EIGHT

GINA could barely contain her panic as Marco brought the meeting to an end. How could she have been so stupid as to say that? It had been such a simple slip, yet it could cause untold damage. Fortunately there was no opportunity for him to say anything with the other woman there, but she knew that he would have questions later.

Could she lie if he asked her how old Lily was? Add on a couple of years to her daughter's age, perhaps? It would put him off the scent but could she live with herself if she deliberately misled him? She felt guilty enough without adding that to her score sheet.

'If there is anything else you want to ask me, please, don't hesitate, Mrs Daniels. Although Chloe will be moving to the children's ward, as the surgeon who operated on her, I shall still take an interest in her ongoing care.'

'Thank you, Doctor. You've been very kind.' Donna grimaced. 'And it's Miss Daniels, actually. Chloe's dad didn't want anything to do with me when I told him I was pregnant. He's never even seen her, in fact.'

'That's a huge shame.'

Marco didn't say anything more so Gina couldn't tell if the comment had been merely a politeness or a genuine expression of regret. She sighed as she ushered Donna from the room. What did it matter how he felt about Donna's situation? He was bound to feel differently when it came to his own child, wasn't he?

The thought nagged away at her as the morning wore on. Marco called all the staff into the office during a quiet period and formally introduced himself. He gave them a brief summary of his career to date and Gina was surprised to discover that he'd been working overseas for the past few years. She had never expected him to leave Italy, but it appeared he had worked in

Australia and the United States. Even though he downplayed his achievements, no one was left in any doubt that he knew his stuff. As Miles Humphreys sourly remarked when they trooped out of the office, the hospital's board must have thought all their birthdays and Christmases had come together when Marco had applied for the post.

That comment gave rise to a great deal of speculation as to why someone of his calibre would choose to relocate to the less salubrious areas of London. Gina managed to avoid giving a direct answer when her opinion was sought, murmuring something about everyone needing a change of scene. The fact that she had a very good idea why Marco had taken the job wasn't something she intended to share. However, it was added pressure on top of the worry about her slip-up that morning. By the time lunchtime arrived her head was aching from thinking about it.

She'd brought a packed lunch and decided to eat it outside in the hope that the fresh air would do her good. It would also mean that there would be less chance of her running into Marco—a definite inducement.

It was rather chilly outside but Gina found a sheltered spot. There were several other members of staff about, although thankfully nobody attempted to join her. She had just finished her sandwiches when she heard footsteps and looked up to see Marco striding towards her. He stopped when he reached the bench, his face betraying very little as he looked down at her.

'So here you are. I wondered where you had got to when I couldn't find you in the canteen.'

Gina gave a little shrug. 'I felt like some fresh air.'

'Ah, I see. So you weren't trying to avoid me? *Bene.* That makes me feel so much better.'

His tone was silky but she still flushed. Bending, she dug into her bag and found the apple she had brought with her, taking her time as she wiped the skin with a paper tissue. However, if she had harboured any hopes that he would take the hint and leave, she was disappointed.

He sat down beside her, tipping back his head

so that the sun's rays fell on his face. 'It is good to feel the sun on your skin, *si*?'

'Mmm.' Gina bit into the apple, using that as an excuse not to answer. If she didn't encourage him, maybe he would give up, she reasoned.

They sat in silence while she ate. Gina could feel her nerves humming with tension as the seconds ticked past. At any moment she expected him to start asking questions and the prospect was almost worse than it actually happening. In the end, she couldn't stand the suspense any longer. She turned and glared at him.

'What do you want, Marco? I don't know what game you're playing but whatever it is, it won't work.'

'Why do you think that I am playing games?' His tone was still smooth but there was an undercurrent to it that sent a prickle of alarm racing through her.

'Because I can't think of a single reason why you would choose to relocate to this area of London apart from it being some sort of...of *stupid* game!'

'That is not true.' He turned to look at her, his brown eyes holding hers fast. 'I came here to solve a problem.'

'What problem? And how can your being here solve anything?'

'Because it was the only way I could think of to get to the bottom of what happened between us, Gina.' His voice dropped, the rich tones sending a flurry of heat through her veins. 'I need to remember you and me, and what we had.'

'Why? It's history, Marco. What's the point of raking up something that is dead and buried?'

'But is it, Gina? Is it really dead and buried? Or is there still something there, some feelings that refuse to be confined to the past?' He shook his head and she could see the bewilderment in his eyes. 'That's what haunts me. This feeling that what we had isn't over, that it should never have ended in the first place.'

Gina felt tears burn her eyes and blinked them away. How she had longed to hear him say those very words at one time, but not now. It was too late for them to go back and too late for them to try again when it could have such a huge impact on Lily.

'That's not what you said when we broke up.' She laughed harshly, whipping up her anger to help her stay strong. 'I can't remember exactly how you phrased it, but I do know you left me in no doubt that you didn't envisage us having a future together.'

'And what about you, Gina? Was that how you felt?' He reached for her hand, his fingers closing firmly around hers. 'Were you sorry we parted? Did you try to make me see sense? Did you want us to stay together? Maybe I shouldn't ask those questions but I need to know.' He lifted her hand and placed it flat against his chest so that she could feel his heart beating beneath her palm. 'I need to know in here that I did the right thing. For both of us.'

Gina took a deep breath. If she told him the truth, that she would have walked over hot coals if it had meant they could be together, it would invite more questions. Yet if she lied and told him that she was glad they had parted, it would feel

as though she was renouncing the most important decision she had ever made. The reason why
she had refused to consider a termination was
because she had been carrying Marco's child.
Nothing would have induced her to harm it when
she had loved him so much.

'What happened three years ago, Marco, happened. Yes, I was upset but I got over it.' She gave
a little shrug. 'So in a way that proves you were
right to call a halt when you did.'

Marco couldn't believe the pain he felt when
she said that. He realised in a sudden flash of in-
sight how much he had been hoping for a different response. He had wanted her to admit that she
had loved him, that she had wished they could
have stayed together; that she would have done
anything to have made it come true. He had
wanted to hear all that and more. How odd.

'I see,' he said, struggling to deal with the
thought. 'It appears that everything worked out
for the best, then, that both of us were happy with
the outcome.'

'Yes.'

There was a hesitancy in her voice that made him look sharply at her. 'Are you sure about that, Gina?'

'Of course I'm sure. Look, Marco, I understand why this is so important to you.'

'You do?' It was his turn to sound hesitant and he saw her grimace.

'Yes. Losing your memory must have been awful for you. You're bound to want to know the ins and outs of everything that happened in your life. It's only natural.'

Was she right? Was it the fact that he couldn't fill in this gap with any degree of certainty that troubled him? Most of the blanks he could fill in at a guess. A half-remembered conversation could make sense once he reasoned it out, a snippet of a scene could be brought to a logical conclusion. But this was different. He couldn't apply logic to second-guess his emotions.

'Maybe you're right.' He summoned a smile, knowing that he wasn't going to achieve anything more by pushing her.

'I am.'

There was such naked relief in her voice that his senses immediately went on the alert. He realised all of a sudden that he still hadn't broached the subject that now concerned him most of all: her daughter. He placed his hand on her arm when she went to get up. 'If it is true that you believe our affair came to a timely end, Gina, why do I have this feeling that you are afraid of me?'

'Afraid?'

'*Si.* It's the reason why I decided to remain in London. I had the strangest feeling that you were scared of me.'

'That's ridiculous! Why on earth would I be scared of you?'

'I don't know. Maybe it has something to do with your daughter.' Marco knew he was right when he saw her blanch. What he didn't understand was why she was so afraid of him finding out about the child. 'I can tell I'm right,' he began, determined to get to the bottom of the mystery. 'I just need to know why...'

He broke off when he heard a child's excited

voice calling 'Mummy'. The next second a little girl appeared and flung herself at Gina.

'What are *you* doing here?' she exclaimed as she swung the child into her arms.

'She insisted on coming to find you, I'm afraid.'

Marco automatically rose when a woman came to join them. She had two young boys with her, obviously twins, but he barely registered them. His attention was focused on the child, on Gina's daughter. With her blonde hair and delicate features the little girl was the image of Gina…apart from her eyes.

Marco could feel the blood pounding inside his skull as he stared at the child. He had seen eyes that colour before; in fact, he saw them every single morning when he stood in front of the mirror, shaving. They were the exact colour of his, a deep golden-brown.

The pressure inside his head seemed to intensify as the memories suddenly came rushing back, memories of him and Gina, and the time they had spent together in Florence. He remembered it all—how he had felt, how afraid he'd been when he had realised that he was falling in love with her. It was all there inside his head, a jumble of conflicting emotions that would have been more than enough to contend with, but there was something else he now had to deal with, something even more mind-blowing.

He shuddered, feeling the shock reaching deep inside him. Was it possible that Gina's daughter was his daughter too?

CHAPTER NINE

GINA'S heart was pounding as she set Lily down on her feet. How long would it take Marco to work out that Lily was his daughter? He only had to look at her to see that she had his eyes so it shouldn't take him long. If he asked her directly if Lily was his child then she would have to tell him the truth; she couldn't not, couldn't lie about something so important.

'This is a lovely surprise, but what are you doing here?' she asked, hearing the strain in her voice. She shot a wary look at Marco but he wasn't looking at her. He was staring at Lily and she knew—she just knew!—that he had worked it out.

'Charlie fell off the swing and cut his knee. It was quite deep so I brought him into ED,' Amy, the childminder, explained. 'He's ended up with three stitches plus a sticker for being such a brave boy.'

'Wow, you are brave,' Gina agreed when the little boy proudly showed her his sticker.

Amy laughed. 'He and Alfie have a collection of stickers on the wall at home. There's hardly a week goes by without one or other of them hurting themselves! Anyway, as soon as Lily knew we were coming to the hospital, she insisted on seeing you.' Amy glanced from her to Marco and grimaced. 'Sorry. We didn't mean to interrupt.'

'You aren't,' Gina assured her quickly. She introduced Marco, ignoring the speculative look on Amy's face. Whatever her friend was thinking was way off beam! There was nothing going on between her and Marco, or nothing like that, at least.

'We'd better let you get on,' Amy said finally, taking hold of Lily's hand. 'Come on, you lot, it's time we went home.'

Gina gave Lily a kiss and waved them off, wishing that she could go with them. Given the choice, she would take Lily home, lock the door and stay there until all this blew over, only it wasn't going to happen. Marco wasn't going to let her escape without telling him the truth, and her heart quaked at the thought.

'We need to talk,' he said flatly, then stopped when his pager beeped. Unhooking it from his belt, he checked the display. 'I am needed in ED,' he said, cancelling the message with an impatient stab of his finger.

Gina nodded, not trusting herself to speak. She couldn't tell him like this, couldn't blurt out that, yes, he was a father and not have time to tell him anything else, like why she had kept Lily's existence a secret. She needed to explain her reasons, convince him that although he might be right to blame her, he must never blame Lily. Her daughter was the innocent victim in all of this, the one who could get hurt the most.

In the end, Marco didn't utter another word. Swinging round on his heel, he strode back up the path. Gina sank back down onto the bench, her whole body trembling as reaction set in.

She had no idea what would happen next but he wouldn't let the matter rest here.

Would he demand to see Lily once it was confirmed that she was his daughter? Or would he be less interested in the child than in the fact that he had solved the mystery that had brought him back here? The truth was that she didn't know how he would react. They had never discussed having children so she had no idea if he hoped to have some of his own one day.

In fact, now that she thought about it, she had no idea if he already *had* a child, maybe more than one, a family even. Their affair had been so brief and so intense that they hadn't delved into each other's pasts. Just being together had been enough and whatever had gone before hadn't mattered. Or so she had thought. Now, however, she found herself wondering if the reason why Marco hadn't asked about her past or told her about his was because he hadn't been interested. She had been merely an eager and willing bedmate, nothing more.

* * *

Marco finished conferring with the young F1 doctor from ED and bade her a brisk goodbye. His opposite number from ED was in a meeting, which was why he had been paged. On his recommendation, the motorcyclist would be on his way to Theatre shortly. His diagnosis, that the rapid fall in the man's blood pressure was the result of internal bleeding, had proved correct: a ruptured spleen was to blame.

He had led the younger doctor through his diagnosis a step at a time, making sure she knew what to look for the next time. He had always enjoyed the mentoring side of his job and normally derived a great deal of satisfaction from it. However, all he could think about was Gina and her daughter.

Was the child his? Was it possible that their brief liaison had resulted in the one thing he had assumed he would never have after Francesca died? As he made his way to AAU he realised that he had to find out the truth before he did anything. There was no point building up his hopes when it might not be true. He couldn't face the disappointment. And even if it did turn out that he was the child's father, as he suspected, it wouldn't be plain sailing; there would be many obstacles to overcome, the biggest one being Gina. The fact that she had chosen not to tell him about their daughter was a good indication of how she felt.

Marco's mouth compressed as he entered the ward. Gina was with a patient. She glanced round when he approached the bed and he could see the fear in her eyes and it annoyed him. What did she think he was going to do? Kidnap the child and make off with her?

'I would like a word with you, Sister, after you've finished here,' he said quietly, nodding politely to the young man lying on the bed.

'I could be a while yet, Dr Andretti.'

'There is no rush. I shall wait in the office until you are free. There are some calls I need to make.'

He walked away, unwilling to give her the chance to think up any more excuses. If it was up to her, they would never have this conversation, but he refused to let her off the hook that easily. If the child was his, he needed to know!

Gina delayed as long as she could until she couldn't think of anything else that needed doing. She made her way to the office, her footsteps dragging as she approached the door. She knew what Marco was going to say and knew what her answer must be but that didn't make it any easier. Once she told him the truth about Lily there could be no going back. It was the thought of what would happen that worried her, the fear of the repercussions the next few minutes might have. She couldn't bear to think that Lily might suffer in any way.

The thought gave her a much-needed boost and she pushed open the door. Marco was on the phone and he glanced up when she appeared. Just for a second his eyes met hers and she felt shock course through her when she saw the apprehension they held. Marco was worried about what she would say? Why? Because he knew that Lily was his and hated the idea of having a child or, rather, having a child with *her*?

The thought was so painful that she flinched and she saw him frown. He curtly ended the conversation and replaced the receiver in its rest. His voice was harsh when he spoke, the richly accented tones grating in a way she had never heard before.

'There is no point dragging this out, Gina. We both know what I want to ask you, so is it true? Am I the father of your child?'

'Yes.' Her voice came out as little more than a croak and she cleared her throat. 'Yes. You are Lily's father.'

'Lily.' He repeated the name as though he was testing it out and that surprised her. Given the circumstances, she wouldn't have expected him to pay any heed to her daughter's name, but obviously it meant something to him. 'Why did you decide to call her Lily?'

'Because I like the name and it seemed to suit her,' she explained, wondering why she felt so touched by his reaction. 'She was so tiny and so perfect when she was born—just like a little flower.'

'I see.' He stood up and walked to the window, his back towards her so that she couldn't see his face. 'It is a very pretty name.'

'I…I'm glad you like it.' Gina knew it was ridiculous to say that. What difference would it have made if he had hated Lily's name? And yet she couldn't deny how good it felt to know that she had done something he approved of.

'I do. I like it very much. Given the choice, I may even have chosen it for her myself, but I never had that choice, did I?' He swung round and she saw the anger that blazed in his eyes. 'You decided that I didn't have the right to help you choose our daughter's name or anything else!'

'I did what I thought was best,' she replied hoarsely, stunned by the speed of the onslaught.

'And that makes it right, does it?' His voice was laced with contempt. 'You decided not to tell me that you were pregnant with my child because you deemed it the *best* thing to do?'

'I did try to tell you! I tried to phone you and even wrote you a letter.'

'Really?'

'Yes, really.' She glared at him. 'When I couldn't reach you by phone and my letter was returned, I realised that you weren't interested.'

'Did it never occur to you that I might not have received your calls or your letter?'

'No, it didn't. As far as I knew, you were still in Florence. I had no idea that you'd moved away to work.'

'You could have found out, though. Someone at the hospital could have told you where I was, if you'd asked.' He smiled thinly. 'But you didn't ask, did you, Gina? You were more than happy to let me live in ignorance of the fact that I was to be a father.'

'Yes, I was.' She stood up straighter, refusing to let him see how much it hurt to have him speak to her that way. 'You'd made your feelings very clear when we broke up, Marco. Although I was going to tell you that I was pregnant, I had no intention of asking you for anything.' She shrugged. 'Maybe I could have tracked you down if I'd tried harder but I did what I thought was in everyone's best interests.'

'How? How can it be in my best interest not to know that I have a child? How can it be in Lily's best interest to grow up not knowing her father? You must forgive me if I appear particularly stupid, Gina, but I fail to see how anyone could benefit from your lies except you.'

'Me?'

'*Si.*' He gave a very expressive shrug. 'We'd had an affair and gone our separate ways. When you found out you were pregnant, I imagine it came as a shock. After all, we had taken precautions. A child was never on the agenda and yet there you were, expecting my baby.

'I imagine you thought about having a termination but in the end decided not to go through with it for whatever reasons. However, deciding that you wanted to keep the baby didn't mean that you wanted me to be involved. I was well out of the picture by then. You had probably moved on to someone else, so why muddy the waters?'

'It wasn't like that!'

'Then what was it like? Come on, Gina, I'm longing to hear why you decided to cut me out of our child's life.'

Gina opened her mouth to reply but just then there was a knock on the door and Julie appeared. She shot a wary glance at them and it was obvious that she had sensed the tension.

'Sorry, but the woman in bay three is kicking up a fuss. She's threatening to discharge herself if she isn't moved to a ward.'

'I'll have a word with her,' Gina said quickly. She glanced at Marco. 'Is that all, Dr Andretti?'

'For now.' Marco strode around the desk. He paused as he drew level with her. 'We shall continue this conversation later.' He stormed out of his office without a backward glance.

It sounded distinctly like a threat and obviously appeared that way to Julie because her mouth dropped open. 'What on earth is going on?' she demanded. 'How have you managed to get into our Italian stallion's bad books so quickly?'

'Don't ask,' Gina replied grimly as she made her way to the ward. She managed to calm down the patient but it was worrying to know that the situation was impacting on her work. If she and Marco were to continue this discussion, it would need to be outside working hours.

The thought wasn't exactly comforting. Given the choice, she would have avoided going anywhere near him again that day, but she didn't have a choice. She would have to arrange to meet him on neutral ground, find out what he wanted, and proceed from there. If Amy would mind Lily that evening, maybe they could sort something out. One thing was certain: the sooner she knew what his intentions were with regard to Lily, the happier she would be.

Marco knew that he had allowed his emotions to get the better of him and hated the thought that he appeared to have so little control. Normally, he viewed each and every problem in the same calm and rational fashion, but he was unable to do that in this instance. Not only had he remembered what Gina had meant to him but he'd found out that he was a father! It was no wonder that his emotions were in turmoil.

He sighed. He needed to calm down and think about what he had learned before he did anything. It was just that Gina's claim to have withheld the fact that he had a daughter had been in his best interests had annoyed him intensely. It took two people to create a child and two people to raise it. Gina must really hate him to have deprived him of all knowledge of his child.

It was incredibly painful to face that fact, especially when he recalled the way she had felt at one time. Gina had been in love with him but he had destroyed any feelings she'd had for him when he had ended their relationship. The thought nagged away at him as the afternoon wore on and he was glad that he was kept busy, monitoring both AAU and ED. When five o'clock arrived, he decided to go up to the admin. department to collect his ID and all the other paperwork he was lacking. He had just summoned the lift when he heard someone calling his name and glanced round to see Gina hurrying towards him.

She got right to the point. 'It's obvious that we need to talk, Marco, so I suggest we meet tonight and try to sort things out.'

'That seems like a good idea to me,' he agreed, wondering if this was really an olive branch or another attempt to sideline him. He sighed inwardly. They would get nowhere if he approached the matter with such a cynical attitude. 'Where do you suggest we meet? I'm afraid I don't know very many places in this part of London.'

'Maybe it would better if we met somewhere more central,' she said with a frown that made her brow pucker in the most adorable way.

Marco was hard-pressed not to reach out and smooth away the tiny furrows but he knew it would be a mistake to blur the boundaries. He had to behave as impersonally as she was, treat this as a business matter and nothing more. 'How about my apartment, then? It's central and there's a tube station five minutes away.'

'I'm not sure if that's a good idea,' she began, then stopped when his brows rose. A wash of colour ran up her face as she glared at him. 'Your apartment will be fine. Shall we make it seven o'clock?'

'Seven is fine with me,' he replied evenly. Was she worried about what might happen if she came to his flat? he wondered. Afraid that their business discussion might turn into something else? Pictures of them lying naked together in his bed suddenly flooded his head and he had to breathe deeply before he continued.

'Use the entry phone and I'll buzz you in. My apartment is on the fifteenth floor so you'll need to take the lift. I'll wait for you in the hallway.'

'Fine.'

He told her the address then stepped into the lift. Gina had already disappeared before the doors closed and he sighed. It was obvious that she didn't view the coming meeting with any enthusiasm. As far as she was concerned, it was a necessary evil. Maybe he should feel the same but there was no escaping the fact that he was looking forward to seeing her that night and not just because he wanted to learn more about his daughter.

Unbidden the image of them lying together in his bed came rushing back and he groaned. It wasn't a memory from the past he was recalling; that would have been just about acceptable. What he was seeing now hadn't happened. He knew that because the bed they were lying in was the bed in his apartment, not the one at the Villa Rosa that they had shared. These images in his head were projections into the future, something he *wanted* to happen.

Just admitting it worried him. Marco knew that if he made love to Gina now it would be different, that *he* would feel differently. Three years ago he had still been grieving for Francesca, still felt angry about losing her, but the accident had changed things and now he had come to terms with what had happened. When...*if*... he made love to Gina again it would be without the shadow of Francesca hanging over him. He would be free of all restraints, free to follow his heart. Free to get hurt. Only this time the pain would be even worse because he had more to lose: Gina *and* his daughter.

CHAPTER TEN

IT WAS a few minutes after seven when Gina arrived at the building where Marco rented an apartment. She pressed the entry button then glanced around. This part of London was one of the most expensive in terms of property. She knew that the rent on an apartment in this area would be as much as her monthly salary. Marco must be extremely well off if he could afford to live in such an exclusive location.

'*Si?*'

She swung round when she heard his voice coming through the speaker. 'It's me,' she said shortly, wondering why the thought unsettled her. The difference in their lifestyles had never bothered her before. She had stayed at his home in Florence and was well aware of how beautiful the villa was with its antique furniture and air of restrained luxury. She had never really thought about it before, but for some reason the contrast between how she and Marco lived suddenly made her feel uneasy.

'*Bene.* I shall unlock the door. Cross the reception area and use the right-hand lift. It stops outside my apartment.'

Gina did as she was told and a few minutes later stepped out into a smartly decorated hallway. Marco was waiting for her and he smiled politely as he ushered her towards one of the doors that opened onto that floor.

'This way,' he said, placing his hand lightly at the small of her back as he guided her inside.

Gina stepped away from him as soon as they were in the apartment, making a great production out of unbuttoning her coat to avoid having him touch her again. Maybe it was nerves but her skin seemed to be tingling in the strangest way where his hand had rested.

'Let me take that for you.'

He took her coat and hung it up in the closet beside the front door then led the way to the sitting room. Gina gasped when she was confronted by the most spectacular view. One entire wall was made of glass and the view across the river towards the Houses of Parliament was stunning.

'The view is the reason why I decided to take this apartment,' he said softly beside her. 'It is magnificent. *Si?*'

'It is.'

She moved away when she felt her skin break out in tingles again. Crossing the room, she sat down on one of the two huge chocolate-brown leather sofas that formed an L-shape in the centre of the room. Her whole flat would fit into this one room with space to spare, she thought wryly.

'I rented the place fully furnished,' Marco told her as he sat down on the other sofa. He shrugged as he reached for the glass cafetière standing on the coffee table. 'It is a little bare for my taste but as I shall only be living here for a limited time, I can put up with it.'

'So you're not planning on staying in England,' she said quickly.

'I wasn't. My contract is for six months.

Although there is an option to extend it, I was planning on returning to Italy at the end of that time.' He poured coffee into two china mugs. 'However, that was before I found out about Lily. Obviously that changes things.'

Gina bit her lip, unsure what to say. Assuring Marco that he shouldn't change his plans because of their daughter might cause him to dig in his heels and do just that. It was going to be difficult enough to cope with having him around for six whole months, but if it was for longer... Well!

The thought of their lives being entwined for many years to come wasn't something she had considered before. However, if he insisted on playing a role in Lily's life then he would play a major role in her life too. She picked up her cup, determined to control the panic that flowed through her. She would deal with his presence in her life if she had to; she really would!

'I assume from your silence that you aren't happy at the thought of me changing my plans because of our daughter.' He shrugged when she glanced up. 'I am sorry if you feel that way,

Gina, because it will make life more difficult for all of us.'

'There is no way that I will allow you to upset Lily!'

'And there is no way that I wish to do so.' His tone was so sharp that she flinched. He leant forward and she could see the determination on his face. 'Upsetting *our* daughter isn't part of my plan. I am just as anxious as you are that Lily shouldn't suffer in any way from all of this.'

Gina knew she should have been reassured but she resented the fact that he thought he had a claim on her precious child. She and Lily had managed perfectly well without him so far and they would have continued to do so if fate hadn't brought him into their lives.

'In that case, the best thing you can do is to leave.' She stared back at him, wishing she had a magic wand to make him disappear. She didn't want him upsetting Lily. She didn't want him upsetting *her*.

The thought that Marco still possessed the power to disturb her wasn't one she welcomed and she glared at him. 'Lily is perfectly happy the way she is. However, if you insist on involving yourself in her life then it's bound to unsettle her.'

'That's your opinion and it seems to me that you have a rather jaundiced view of me, Gina.'

His tone was even but she could hear the underlying hurt it held and couldn't help feeling a little guilty. Maybe he genuinely believed that it was right to involve himself in their child's life but how long would he continue to feel like that? His interest in Lily would probably wane as quickly as it had arisen and she would be left trying to console a disappointed little girl. The thought helped her harden her heart.

'If I have a jaundiced view of you, Marco, it's all down to past experience. I hate to say this, but you don't have a good track record when it comes to being dependable. In fact, I've never met anyone who blows hot and cold as quickly as you do.'

'Hot and cold? I'm sorry but I am not sure what you mean.'

He leant forward, his brown eyes holding hers

fast. Gina felt her breath catch when she found herself trapped by his searching gaze. It had been a long time since he had looked at her with such intensity, as though her every thought mattered to him, she thought wonderingly.

'Gina?' He prompted her to answer and she jumped.

'I…I meant that you seem to change your mind on a whim. One minute you appear to be very keen on something and the next it's the last thing you want anything to do with.'

'Something or *someone*?' he put in quietly.

She shrugged. 'If you want the truth, yes. One minute we seemed to be as close as two people could be and the next you didn't want anything to do with me. Is it any wonder that I don't trust you when it comes to Lily?'

Marco wasn't sure how to answer. How could he explain why he had chosen to break up with her without revealing too much? Would it be wise to admit that he had been on the brink of falling in love with her and that the thought had terrified him when he had sensed that she wouldn't want to hear it?

He stared at her for a long moment, letting his eyes drink in the delicate beauty of her face. It wasn't just that her features were so perfect, but the inner sweetness beneath the outer beauty. Gina was everything a man could want and he had given her up because he had been afraid of getting hurt. He took a deep breath, aware that the problem hadn't changed. He was still afraid, especially as he had even more to lose this time.

'There's nothing I can say apart from promising you that I will never let Lily down.' He cleared his throat, aware that his emotions were far too near the surface. 'Just because we split up, it doesn't mean that I will reject Lily. She's my daughter and I swear on my life that I shall do everything possible to make sure she is safe and happy if you will let me.'

Gina didn't say a word as she stared down at her hands. He could tell how difficult it was for her and the thought of what she must be going through was too much. Leaning forward, he laid his hand over hers, willing her to believe him.

'I mean it, Gina. You really can trust me this time. I promise you.'

'It's easy to say that now but you could change your mind.' She removed her hands from his grasp. 'The time may come when it isn't convenient to have a child around.'

'Convenient?' He frowned, hiding his chagrin at the way she had drawn away. She had made it plain that she didn't want him to touch her and it stung to know how she felt when he felt so very differently.

He clamped down on the re-run of those images he'd had earlier in the day, the ones that involved him and Gina in his bed, and forced himself to focus on what she had said. So what if she never slept with him again; what did it matter? He would survive as he had survived in the three years since they had parted. 'Why should having a child cause me any inconvenience?'

'Because a lot of women wouldn't be happy at

the thought of their husband or lover having a child from a previous relationship.'

It took a second for him to grasp her meaning and a few more before he could work out what to reply. Maybe it was silly but did he really want to admit that there had been no other women in his life since they had parted? 'That isn't an issue, I assure you.'

'Maybe not at the moment but who knows what will happen in the future?' She shrugged. 'You could meet someone and find that you neither want nor have the time to spend with Lily. It happens, believe me.'

'It won't happen in this instance,' he insisted.

'If you say so.'

It was obvious that she didn't believe him and he knew that he had to convince her he was telling the truth if they were to get anywhere at all. 'Yes, I do. I am not interested in having a relationship with another woman, Gina. I never was interested even when I met you.'

'I see. Well, that answers one question.' Her eyes glistened with tears as she stood up. 'I always did wonder why you got involved with me and now I know. You just wanted someone you could have sex with and I fitted the bill.' She gave a bitter little laugh. 'Thanks for that, Marco. I'm under no illusions now!'

She snatched her bag off the couch and headed for the door but there was no way he would let her go thinking that. He hurried after her, catching hold of her arm to bring her to a halt. 'Wait! That wasn't what I meant. You got it all wrong.'

'I don't think so. Now, if I can have my coat...' She turned towards the wall, searching for the concealed catch that unlocked the closet door.

Marco reached past her and opened the door, lifting out her coat, although he didn't give it to her. 'You've got it wrong, Gina,' he repeated. 'It was never just sex. You must know that.'

'Oh, please! Spare me the platitudes. Why not call a spade a spade and be done with it?'

He smiled faintly although there was nothing amusing about the situation. To know that she was hurting this much was almost more than he could bear. 'I assume we aren't discussing gardening implements, *si*? In that case, if you want the truth, that's what I am giving you.'

He turned her to face him, feeling her resistance in the stiffness of her body. 'It was never just sex between us. It was far more than that.' He cupped her chin with his hand so that she was forced to look at him. 'What I felt for you, Gina, was so much more than sex that I was terrified. That's why I broke up with you. Because I was afraid.'

'Afraid? Of what? What could you possibly have been afraid of?'

Her voice echoed with disbelief and hurt, and he couldn't bear it. Bending, he placed his mouth over hers and kissed her, a kiss that held a plea for understanding. Maybe he was making a mistake but he needed to convince her that he was telling the truth: she needed to believe it!

He drew back, seeing the shock that shimmered in her eyes, yet it was the fact that he could also see the awareness they held too that was the biggest surprise of all. Gina had been stirred by his kiss, even enjoyed it, and the thought made him feel ten feet tall.

'Of getting hurt again.' He paused, battling to contain his emotions because this wasn't the time to get carried away. He needed to be honest with her and hope that it would help him gain her trust with regard to Lily. 'Like I'd been hurt when I lost Francesca.'

Gina could hear a rushing in her head. It was so loud that it blotted out everything else. She could see Marco speaking to her but she couldn't hear what he was saying. When he led her back into the sitting room and sat her down, she didn't protest.

She had never expected him to kiss her and certainly never expected to feel that familiar surge of desire rise up inside her. However, the moment his lips had claimed hers, she had been transported back to the days when he had been her whole world and she had thought she'd been his, only that hadn't been true. It couldn't have been, not when he had spoken about another woman in such a way.

'Here, drink this.'

He pushed a glass into her hand and she obediently took a sip of the liquid then coughed when the spirit hit the back of her throat. He took the glass from her and went to pat her on the back but she moved out of his way. She couldn't bear to feel his hands on her. She had a feeling that she might break down and that was the last thing she could afford to do. It appeared the situation was worse than she had imagined. Now there was another woman to add to the equation, a woman who, apparently, had meant everything to him. It took all her courage to ask the question but she needed to know.

'Who exactly is Francesca?'

He glanced down at the glass he was holding and when he looked up there was a bleakness about his expression that made her heart ache. 'Francesca is…was my wife.'

CHAPTER ELEVEN

'YOUR wife!'

Marco saw the shock on Gina's face. He took a deep breath, knowing that he had to get this over with as quickly as possible. '*Si*. She died four years ago.'

'*Died*? But how? Why?'

She stopped, obviously equally stunned by this new revelation, and he sighed, aware that he wasn't handling things very well. 'It was a tragic accident. Francesca was out shopping and a car swerved to avoid a child who ran into the road. It mounted the pavement and knocked Francesca down.'

He paused, waiting for the familiar rush of pain he always felt whenever he spoke about what had happened and yet, oddly, all he felt was sadness at such a cruel waste of a life. He cleared his throat.

'There was nothing anyone could do. Francesca was crushed against a wall and she was killed outright.'

'How awful! I don't know what to say...' She tailed off, biting her lip as she struggled to find some words of comfort to offer him.

'There is nothing anyone can say, Gina. It was a terrible accident, the sort of thing you read about in the newspapers and never imagine will happen to someone you know.'

'You must have been devastated.'

'I was. I couldn't believe it at first. I kept expecting to wake up and find that it had been some sort of awful dream. It took me a long time to accept that Francesca wasn't coming back.'

'It must have been so hard for you, Marco.' Tears shimmered in her eyes as she reached out and touched his hand.

'It was.'

He turned his hand over, his fingers closing around hers, feeling the jolt of awareness that shot through him when his skin made contact with hers. That he was capable of feeling like that when they were discussing such a terrible period in his life shocked him. It was difficult to concentrate but he knew that he had to tell her everything in the hope that it would help.

'It was the sheer unexpectedness of what happened that was the worst thing of all. If Francesca had been ill, I would have had time to prepare myself, but with an accident like that...' He stopped, not trusting himself to continue. His emotions were already raw and it would take very little to let all the shock and horror he had kept bottled up pour out. Whilst it might be healing for him, it wouldn't help Gina. She had enough to deal with without him burdening her with this.

'It was a very difficult time,' he said finally, 'but I had my work and that helped me get through it.'

'I'm glad, but still...'

She paused, obviously expecting him to say something else, but he stayed silent. This wasn't a bid for her sympathy but a chance to explain his actions. Maybe then she would understand why he had felt the need to end their affair, accept that it hadn't been a lack of feeling that had driven him to do so but, rather, the fear of feeling too much.

His heart began to race as he recalled how desperate he had felt three years ago. He had been on the brink of falling in love with Gina and he'd been terrified of what it could mean. That was why he had pushed her away, because he'd been afraid of getting hurt again if anything happened to her.

What if he started to feel that way again? he wondered. What would he do then? How could he walk away when they had a child to consider?

Marco stood up, feeling his stomach churning as he went over to the window. He couldn't turn his back on his daughter. He couldn't and wouldn't abandon her, yet the more involved he became with Lily, the more involved he would become with Gina. Somehow he had to take control of the situation, minimise the damage it could cause for all of them. As long as he recognised his own vulnerability, he would cope. He had to.

He sat down again, deliberately removing any trace of emotion from his voice. 'Whilst what

I've told you obviously had a bearing on what happened three years ago, we need to focus on the future now. I meant what I said about wanting to be involved in Lily's life, Gina. Maybe you find it hard to believe but it's true. Our daughter's welfare is my only concern from now on.'

Gina knew that he was waiting for her to say something and struggled to find the right words. He sounded so composed and she envied him that. She took a quick breath, trying not to think about what he had said about his reasons for ending their relationship…

He must have really felt something for you if he'd been afraid to let matters continue, a small voice whispered inside her head.

She closed her mind to that tantalising thought, determined that it wasn't going to distract her. It was Lily's future at stake now and nothing was more important than that. 'I hope you mean that, Marco. I hope it isn't just…well, a reaction to finding out that you have a child.'

'A reaction? I'm not sure what you mean.'

'Obviously, it was a shock to learn that you

have a daughter. It's understandable if you feel you're responsible for Lily in the first rush of enthusiasm. However, I understand if you have second thoughts.'

'I shall not have second thoughts.' His face closed up as he stared coldly back at her. 'If the child is mine, there is no question that I intend to be involved in her life.'

'*If* Lily is yours? That implies you have doubts. Do you, Marco?'

Gina wasn't sure why she felt so hurt. After all, it was only natural that he would want to be sure that Lily was his child. In fact, it could work to her advantage because he would be less keen to play an active role in Lily's life if he doubted his paternity. And yet the thought that he might think she would lie about something so important stung.

'No. I don't have any doubts whatsoever.' His gaze was level. 'If you say that Lily is my child then I believe you.'

It was the affirmation she wanted and yet she

found herself pushing him for more. 'Even though I failed to tell you about her?'

He shrugged. 'They are two separate issues. Whilst I still believe you could have tried harder to contact me, I don't believe you would try to pass off another man's child as mine. Lily is my daughter, isn't she?'

He challenged her to deny it but there was no way that Gina would make matters worse by doing that. 'Yes, she's your child, Marco. There is no question about that.'

'*Bene.* Now all we need to decide is when I can see her. Obviously, I don't want to wait. I've lost enough time as it is, so I suggest we arrange to meet this weekend. You can bring Lily here or I can come to your home.'

'This weekend! But that's just a few days away. It's far too soon to see her this weekend.'

'That is your view, Gina. My view is that the sooner I meet her, the sooner we shall get to know one another.' His tone was unyielding. 'I realise that it will be hard for the little one to understand who I am at first. I assume you haven't mentioned me to her—isn't that so?'

Gina nodded, wondering if he could tell how guilty she felt. She hadn't told Lily about him because there'd seemed no point. They weren't going to see him so there had been no reason to confuse Lily by telling her about a father she would never meet. It had seemed so sensible before and yet she felt awful for deliberately cutting him out of her daughter's life.

'I thought not. In that case, I suggest we don't confuse her by telling her who I am to begin with. Let her get used to me and then, when she has accepted me as part of her life, we can tell her that I'm her daddy.'

It made sense, although she was surprised that he was willing to wait. She had assumed that he would want to rush in, claim Lily as his own and make a fuss about being her father. It made her wonder if she had misjudged him and that if she had done so with regard to this then perhaps she had misjudged him in other matters too.

The thought was more than a little unsettling.

Gina forced it to the back of her mind. 'That seems the most sensible thing to do,' she agreed. Marco might be keen to take on his new role as a father but it didn't mean he was interested in resuming his old role in her life. Their affair was over and he had made that clear. The fact that they had a child was the only thing that united them now.

'I'm glad you agree.' He suddenly smiled. 'It appears that we can work together if we try, doesn't it?'

'So it seems.' Gina shrugged, hoping he couldn't tell how on edge she felt. She should be pleased they had managed to reach an amicable solution, and she was. However, she couldn't deny that part of her hated to think that the only thing which bound them now was Lily.

'*Bene.* Now all that is left to do is to arrange a time and a place where we can meet. Where do you suggest?'

Marco was all business. If he felt even a flicker of regret that their affair was well and truly relegated to the past, it didn't show, Gina thought, then wondered why it bothered her so much. She forced herself to emulate his businesslike tone so that he wouldn't have any inkling of how confused she felt.

'I suggest we go to the park. It will be less formal that way and Lily won't feel so daunted about meeting a stranger.'

Marco's lips compressed at the word 'stranger' but he didn't challenge her. 'If that's what you feel is best then that is what we shall do.'

They agreed to meet in Hyde Park at eleven on the Saturday morning then Gina stood up. 'I'll have to go. Lily is usually in bed by now and I need to get her home.'

'Who's minding her tonight?' he asked, holding her coat so she could slip her arms into the sleeves.

'Amy,' Gina replied, struggling to get the coat on as quickly as possible. She knew it was silly but just feeling him there, behind her, made her feel all keyed up. She shoved her hand down the left sleeve, grimacing when her watch strap snagged on a loose thread in the lining. She tried to work it free but it was well and truly stuck. Marco frowned as he peered over her shoulder.

'What's the matter?'

'My watch has caught on a thread,' she said, trying to force her hand down the sleeve.

'Careful! You will rip the lining.' He stepped in front of her and took hold of her arm so he could slide his hand inside the sleeve. 'Ah, yes, I can feel it now.'

He inched his hand further up the sleeve and Gina felt her breath catch. By necessity they were standing so close that she could smell the tang of soap that came off his skin, feel the heat of his body, and it was such a heady mix that all her senses suddenly went on the alert. It was sheer torture to feel his fingers smoothing over her skin and not respond. Even though there was nothing overtly sexual about his actions, she could feel desire pooling in the pit of her stomach, feel every nerve ending quivering with anticipation…

'Ah! That seems to have solved the problem.'

He removed his hand and stepped back. Gina blinked as all the emotions that had been building up inside her suddenly drained away. She took a quick breath as she pushed her hand out of the sleeve. She didn't want to make love with him. It was the last thing she wanted!

'Thank you.' She hurried into the hall, reaching for the catch to open the door, but he was ahead of her.

'I can tell that you're in a hurry so I won't keep you,' he said as he opened the door for her. 'Thank you for coming tonight, Gina, and for being so reasonable. It has helped to set my mind at rest.'

'I'm not sure I understand what you mean,' she said, frowning up at him.

'I was worried in case our past relationship would make it impossible for us to work together.' His voice dropped, the richly accented tones sounding more pronounced than ever as he continued. 'I know I hurt you and I am truly sorry about that. But I hope you understand now why I couldn't allow our relationship to continue.'

'Because you were afraid of getting hurt again.' She took a quick breath, knowing it was foolish to ask but unable to resist. 'And could that have happened, Marco? Was I really such a threat to you?'

'Yes.' He kissed her gently on the cheek and his eyes were very dark when he drew back. 'I knew you had the power to turn my life upside down and that is the one thing I shall never risk. I don't want to fall in love again, Gina. I refuse to allow it to happen. I just hope that we can move on and become friends as well as good parents to our daughter.'

'Ye-yes, of course.' Gina managed to smile before she swung round and hurried out of the door. She summoned the lift, praying it wouldn't take long to arrive. When Marco bade her goodbye she somehow managed to respond. Within seconds she was exiting the building and hurrying along the street but realised that she was heading in the wrong direction.

She retraced her steps, averting her eyes as she passed the apartment block. No doubt Marco was congratulating himself that everything had been sorted out with so little fuss. He was determined not to get emotionally involved, or at least not with her.

Gina felt a wave of pain wash over her. Although he claimed that he had been on the verge of falling in love with her, was it true? She had loved him so much that nothing could have persuaded her to give him up, neither bad memories nor fear of what the future held. Her love for him had transcended everything else; he had been all that had mattered. But he hadn't felt that way, had he?

He had examined his feelings, decided that he wasn't prepared to risk getting hurt, and acted accordingly. It made her wonder if he really understood what love was all about. Not that it mattered now, of course. Not when he had made it clear that their relationship was going to be strictly that of friends and parents.

She took a steadying breath. She had to accept that she and Marco were never going to be lovers.

CHAPTER TWELVE

MARCO spent a restless evening after Gina left. Although he was relieved that they had managed to sort things out so satisfactorily, he couldn't rid himself of the feeling that he had made a mess of things. He went over what had happened a dozen times or more but he couldn't pinpoint what was causing him to feel so edgy. It was just a feeling he had that he had said something to upset her and it worried him.

Maybe he would ask her in the morning if everything was all right, he mused as he got into bed. And maybe he wouldn't, he decided as he switched off the light. If they were to stick to their roles as parents and friends, it would be better not to introduce any other issues into the equation.

AAU was frantically busy when he arrived the

following morning. He was surprised to discover that many of the patients who had been due to be transferred were still on the unit, including little Chloe Daniels. He waited until Gina had finished dealing with a new admission and called her into the office.

'What's going on? Why are so many of yesterday's patients still here? Chloe Daniels should have gone straight to Paediatrics after she left Recovery.'

'There's a problem in Paeds as well as in Women's Surgical. Water's been leaking from the storage tanks on the roof and it's brought down part of the ceiling on that floor. Some patients have been transferred to other hospitals, but they decided not to move Chloe as she'd just had surgery and sent her back to us.'

'I see.' Marco frowned as he considered how this would affect them. 'How long will it be before everything is back to normal?'

'No one seems to know.' Gina sighed. 'If it's just a matter of clearing up and replacing the ceiling then it could be a week, but if the damage is more serious it will take longer.'

'And in the meantime we're going to be pushed for space. Are there any side rooms that can be made available?'

'There's two beds in the high dependency unit which we can use. And there's another in the room we use for any patients requiring barrier nursing. That's it, though.'

'So that makes three plus any that become available throughout the day,' he concluded.

Although it was annoying to know that they would be put under extra pressure, it was a relief to turn his attention to a less personal problem. It had taken him a long time to fall asleep and when he had, his dreams had been filled with images of Gina. It was as though now he had remembered their affair, his memory was more acute than ever. He could recall in vivid detail every day he had spent with her: each hour, each minute, each second. It had been such a magical time that it was hard to believe he'd had the strength to let go.

He hastily dismissed that thought, knowing how dangerous it was. 'I want you to ring round all the wards and make it clear that we won't be able to keep patients here once they have been referred to a consultant.'

'They're not going to be happy,' Gina warned him.

'Probably not but there is nothing we can do about it. We need to free up beds for those who require urgent treatment. In other words, we have to get back to basics and make sure the department is used for acute admissions only. I noticed yesterday that some cases don't fall into that category. I'll have a word with Tom Petty, the ED consultant, and make sure he's aware of the problems we're facing. If we work together, we should be able to find a solution.'

Gina nodded, trying not to think about the other problem Marco had been so keen to find a solution to. She sighed as she followed him out of the office. She had spent the best part of the night thinking about what had happened in his apartment. Even when he had admitted how devastated he had been after his wife had died, he had still remained in control. Add to that the way he had been able to rationalise his feelings for her and it all added up to a man who rarely allowed himself to be led by his emotions.

Was that a good or a bad thing with regard to Lily? she wondered. Would he be able to detach himself as easily from his own child? Her biggest fear was that Lily would grow attached to him only to be let down at some point. Marco may have managed to allay her fears the previous evening but during the night they had come flooding back. She wouldn't allow him to break Lily's heart as he had broken hers!

'Marco, just a moment,' she said hurriedly as he went to walk away. She felt her pulse quicken when he turned and tried to ignore the rush of blood that ran through her veins. The fact that she was so aware of him didn't matter. It was the damage he could cause to her precious daughter that was important.

'About Saturday and you meeting Lily, I don't think it's a good idea after all. I think we should wait a couple of weeks. It will give me time to prepare her and, more importantly, give *you* time to think about what you're doing.' She gave a little shrug when he didn't say anything. 'There's no point jumping in, feet first, and then regretting it.'

'So you still think that I shall have second thoughts.'

'I think it's extremely likely given your track record.'

'What happened between us has no bearing whatsoever on my relationship with our daughter.'

'In that case, it doesn't matter if you meet Lily this weekend or next.'

'It matters to me.' He stepped closer, his eyes holding hers fast. 'And it matters to Lily as well. The longer it takes before I meet her, the harder it will be to establish a relationship. So if you're planning on not turning up on Saturday, I suggest you think really hard about what you are doing. I don't want to fight with you, Gina, but I will if you try to stop me seeing my child. Understand?'

He didn't wait for a reply. Gina took a shaky breath as he strode away. He had sounded so angry that it made her wonder how she had ever imagined they could work together.

'Hey, are you OK? You've not had another run-in with the gorgeous Marco, have you?'

Gina jumped when Julie tapped her on the arm. She dredged up a smile. 'Just a minor difference of opinion.'

'Hmm, interesting.' Julie grinned at her. 'There's definitely a vibe when you two are together. I'm not the only one who's noticed it either. Still, they say that love and hate are two sides of the same coin, don't they?'

'Rubbish! It's just a clash of personalities. I'm sure things will even out once Dr Andretti gets used to our way of doing things.'

'Pity!' Julie heaved an exaggerated sigh. 'Here was I thinking that you had finally met a man who pushes your buttons. You're too young to be on your own, Gina. You need love, romance, *sex*!'

Gina laughed. 'I shall bear that in mind. However, you can strike Marco off the list. Been there, done that and thrown away the T-shirt, thank you.'

'What! Did I hear you right?' Julie gaped at her. 'Are you saying that you two were an item once?'

Gina could have bitten off her tongue. The last thing she needed was for folk to start gossiping. 'That's a bit strong. I met him a while ago in Italy. We went out a few times and that was it. I came back to England and didn't see him again until he was brought in after that accident.'

'You never said anything,' Julie pointed out, and Gina sighed.

'No, I didn't. I know what the grapevine is like in this place and I didn't want everyone making something out of nothing. Marco was just someone I dated, so I hope you won't say anything to the others.'

'My lips are sealed.' Julie fastened an imaginary zip across her mouth. 'I won't say a word, except that I think you might be wrong about him being just someone you went out with. There's obviously something going on between you two. OK, so maybe things didn't go too well in the past, but who knows what could happen in the future, eh?'

Julie winked at her then hurried off to answer a patient's bell. Gina went into the ward and made a list of all the patients who had been referred to other departments. Phoning round took some time and Marco hadn't returned by the time she finished. Whether he was still consulting with Tom Petty in ED, she didn't know and didn't care, she assured herself. Where Marco went and what he did wasn't her concern except when it impacted on Lily. And she had no intention of allowing him to bully her round to his way of thinking. If she decided something wasn't right for her daughter, she would stick to her guns and he could either like it or lump it!

Saturday dawned bright and clear. As Marco stepped out of the shower, he could feel anticipation bubbling inside him. Meeting Lily today was going to be a life-changing experience.

He had always wanted a family, although since Francesca had died, he had never really thought about it. However, now that it was fait accompli, so to speak, he realised how important it was to him. He was excited by the prospect and it could only have been better if he and Gina had been able to provide Lily with a proper home. Children needed both a mother and father, preferably living under the same roof.

He sighed because the likelihood of that happening was nil. Apart from the fact that he had no intention of getting involved with Gina, she would never agree to it. He had really hurt her and although she might be able to accept what he had done eventually, she wasn't there yet. She was still hurt, still angry with him, and it meant that he would have to tread very carefully. Setting up home together wasn't on the cards even for Lily's sake.

It was just gone ten when he arrived at the park and there were already a lot of people about. He strolled along beside the Serpentine, checking his watch frequently so he wouldn't be late. At ten minutes to eleven he headed over to the children's playground, feeling his pulse quicken when he spotted Gina sitting on a bench. At least she had come, he thought as he went to join her.

'*Buon giorno*, Gina. How are you today?'

She turned to look at him and he could see the wariness in her eyes. 'Fine.'

She didn't ask how he was, didn't seem keen to make conversation, in fact, and he sighed. 'We shall get nowhere if you insist on treating me like some kind of pariah. Children are very astute and Lily will soon notice that something is wrong. It isn't fair that you should colour her view of me before I've had a chance to get to know her.'

Heat rushed up her cheeks as she glared at him. 'I have no intention of colouring her view of you! I just need you to understand that once you start this, you can't suddenly change your mind. If this isn't what you really want, Marco...'

'Mummy! Look!'

They both turned when a small voice interrupted them. Marco felt a lump come to his throat as his gaze settled on the little girl. Her blonde hair was caught up into a ponytail, a bright pink bobble that matched her T-shirt holding it in place. She was wearing denim jeans with a pair of miniature trainers on her feet. Marco felt his heart catch when it struck him that if he and Gina had never met then Lily wouldn't be here.

'Here.'

Lily held out her hand and Marco saw that she had a buttercup clutched in her fist. Tears welled into his eyes as he gently took it from her.

'Is this for me, *tesoro*?' he asked, his voice thickening with emotion. *'Grazie.'*

Lily stared at him for a moment then suddenly turned and ran over to the slide. Marco watched as she climbed the steps. He was overwhelmed by what had happened and didn't know how to react. This was his child, his flesh and blood, and meeting her affected him in a way he had never expected.

'She loves the slide and will spend hours on it if you let her,' Gina said quietly beside him.

Marco knew that she had seen his tears yet, oddly, it didn't embarrass him. 'She's beautiful, isn't she? So perfect...' He tailed off, unable to put into words the awe he felt that they had created this precious human being.

'She is but, then, I expect I'm biased.'

She laughed but there was a wobbly note in her voice that told him she was touched by his reaction. Hearing it seemed to release even more emotions inside him and he sighed.

'I never expected to feel so overwhelmed. It's hard to get my head round the idea that if we hadn't met Lily wouldn't be here.' He turned to her. 'Thank you, Gina. I know how inadequate that is, but thank you from the bottom of my heart for giving me something so wonderful and so precious.'

CHAPTER THIRTEEN

IT WAS a magical day. Whether it was Marco's obvious delight in his daughter, or the fact that Lily seemed to accept him without question, Gina wasn't sure, but the day went so well that even her fears were allayed. As they made their way to the café for lunch, she found herself thinking that maybe everything would turn out all right after all. If Marco continued to show this amount of interest in his daughter then surely there was nothing to fear?

'Shall we sit here?' Marco put his hand under her elbow and guided her towards a table near the window.

Gina shivered when she felt the warmth of his fingers on her skin. She bent down to lift Lily out of her pram, glad of the excuse to break the contact. Even though Marco had responded far more favourably than she had expected, it wasn't a reason to allow her emotions to run riot. He would have to do an awful lot more before he cast his spell over her as he had so obviously cast it over their daughter!

The thought sent a shiver down her spine. Gina knew it would be a mistake to go down that route. She fixed a polite smile to her mouth as she turned to him, deeming it safer to stick to practicalities. 'Lily will need a high chair. There's one over there if you wouldn't mind fetching it.'

'Of course.' He bent and tickled the little girl under her chin, making her chuckle. 'One second, *tesoro*, and you shall have your very own seat, *si*?'

Gina sat down, glad of the few seconds' breathing space. Marco had already defined what his role was going to be and she mustn't forget that. The biggest mistake she could make would be to think he might become more to her than Lily's father.

It was a sobering thought but it did the trick. By the time he came back with the high chair, she had herself in hand. She started to rise so that she could strap Lily into the chair but Marco was ahead of her.

'May I do it? It will be good practice for me. I need some hands-on experience about the realities of being a father, don't you think?'

'Of course.'

Gina bit her lip as he lifted Lily off her lap. He swung the little girl above his head, buzzing her cheek with a kiss before he lowered her into the chair. Lily squealed with delight, obviously enjoying every second of the attention. The speed with which the child had accepted him surprised her. Normally, Lily was shy around people she didn't know but there was no hesitancy about her manner with Marco. Did she recognise him on some unconscious level? she wondered. Understand that he was her daddy? If anyone had suggest the idea, she would have dismissed it as nonsense, but having seen how Lily responded to him, it was hard to do so, and it made her feel incredibly guilty. She would have denied Lily the chance to meet Marco if he hadn't reappeared in her life.

'I think that is right.' Marco frowned as he studied the safety harness. 'I can see that I shall have to practise. These things are far more complicated than they appear.'

He gave her a broad smile and she felt her heart leap when she saw the amusement in his eyes. It was obvious that he was having just as much fun as Lily was and it was something she hadn't anticipated. Marco was usually so controlled that it surprised her he should take such delight in the simple task.

'I often think you need a degree to operate all the various pieces of equipment you buy when you have a child. Between the intricacies of unfolding pushchairs and the vagaries of safety harnesses, you need to be an engineer!' she observed lightly.

'Oh, dear. I didn't realise it was so complicated!'

He laughed, drawing the attention of two young women at the next table. Gina saw one of them say something to her friend and had a good idea what it was, not that she blamed her. With his dark Latin looks, Marco was enough to attract any woman's attention.

The thought stung even though she knew it shouldn't have done. She battened it down, knowing that she couldn't allow herself to feel jealous. Marco could date as many women as he liked and it had nothing to do with her! 'I'm sure you'll cope,' she said, doing her best to convince herself that she didn't care a jot what he did.

'And if I don't, I can ask you for help.'

His gaze was warm as it rested on her. Gina felt her heart begin to hammer and deliberately looked away. Picking up the menu, she scanned down the list of dishes on offer. Marco wasn't flirting with her—he was just being friendly. However, it didn't feel like that...

'So what do you want to eat?' He leant over her shoulder so he could read the menu and her heart gave such a huge bounce that she gasped.

'Are you all right?' he asked in concern, bending so that he could look into her face, which only made matters worse.

'I…er…um…banged my knee on the table leg,' she murmured. 'Anyway, I think I'll have a chicken salad.'

'*Bene.* And Lily, what will she have?'

Marco ran a tanned finger down the menu until he reached the children's options. Gina bit her lip as she followed its progress. She mustn't think about all the times he had run his finger down her spine, the gentle touch setting alight every nerve-ending in its path. They were having a simple family lunch, not enjoying the precursor to an afternoon of seduction!

'Fish fingers, chips and peas,' she said quickly. She grimaced when he raised his brows. 'It's her favourite meal. She'd eat it every day if I let her.'

'In that case, fish fingers it is, although hopefully I can persuade her to try pasta one day.' He gave her another warm smile but she was prepared this time and smiled coolly back.

'You can try, although I'm not sure how much success you'll have. Like a lot of children, Lily is very determined when it comes to what she will eat.'

'And there is no point making an issue of it.' Marco nodded. 'You are right, Gina. The more we fuss, the more she will refuse to try new things. I shall remember that.'

He headed to the counter to place their order. Gina shivered. Was it that unconscious use of the word 'we' that troubled her? He seemed to have taken it for granted that they would be enjoying many more outings like this in the future, but would it happen? Would he be content to spend his free time entertaining a small child when he could be doing something more exciting?

It was that same niggling doubt again and until she had laid it to rest, once and for all, she knew that she couldn't relax. She had to be on her guard around him for Lily's sake.

She bit her lip. She had to be on her guard for her own sake too.

By the time three o'clock arrived, it was obvious that Lily was flagging. After lunch, they had returned to the playground where she had played on all the equipment. Marco knew that the sound of her excited laughter was imprinted in his mind. It was one memory that no one could take away from him. In years to come he would look back on this day and know that it marked a milestone in his life.

He glanced at Gina because it wasn't just being with Lily that had made the day so special: it was the way Gina had reacted too. She had allowed him far more leeway than he had expected, letting him push Lily on the swing, spin her on the roundabout, do all the things that a proper father did, in fact. He was suddenly overcome with gratitude that she had made the occasion so easy for him. He turned to her, seeing the question in her eyes when he brought the pushchair to a halt.

'I just want to thank you, Gina, for being so kind. I know you have concerns but you haven't let them show.' He glanced at Lily, tenderness welling up inside him. 'I was wrong to accuse you of trying to colour the little one's view of me because you certainly haven't done that today.'

'I just want her to be happy. That's the only thing that concerns me, Marco.'

'I understand.' He bent and kissed her on the cheek, feeling his pulse leap when he felt the softness of her skin. It took a massive effort of will to draw back but he knew that he mustn't make the mistake of confusing the issue when everything seemed to be going so well. And letting Gina know that he desired her would be a mistake.

His breath caught as he was forced to acknowledge how strong his feelings for her were. He wanted her as much now as he had three years ago and it was scary to know that he felt the same after all this time. He straightened abruptly, forcing a note of lightness into his voice in the hope that it would disguise how he felt. He couldn't resume his affair with her. Even if she was willing, which was doubtful, he couldn't take the risk!

'I'd better let you get off home. From the look of this little one, she should sleep well tonight.'

'I'm sure she will.' Gina gave him a quick smile as they carried on. They reached Lancaster Gate, where she paused. 'We're going to catch the Tube so we'll say goodbye here. Thank you for lunch. It was very kind of you.'

'Thank you for agreeing to meet me,' he said formally. He bent and smiled at a sleepy Lily. '*Ciao, tesoro.* I shall see you again very soon.'

He brushed the child's cheek with his lips then stood up, feeling oddly bereft now that the time had come for them to part. It was on the tip of his tongue to suggest that they came back to his apartment and spend the evening there until he thought better of it. Lily was tired and no doubt Gina needed a breathing space after what must have started out as a stressful day.

'I hope we can do this again soon. I have enjoyed it, Gina. Very much indeed.'

'Lily enjoyed it too.' She gave him another quick smile then pushed the buggy out of the gate. She didn't look back as she hurried across the road and disappeared into the station.

Marco headed home, trying to rid himself of a vague sense of disappointment. So what if Gina hadn't given him any inkling if she had enjoyed the day? At least she hadn't ruled out the chance of it happening again and that was the main thing. He couldn't expect her to be enthusiastic about spending time with him after the way he had behaved three years ago, could he?

He sighed. She must be as wary of him as he was of her, although for very different reasons.

Gina had Monday and Tuesday off and didn't see Marco again until the middle of the following week. She had to admit that she was glad, too. Spending so much time with him had left her feeling very unsettled. Far too many times she found herself going over what had happened at the park. To an outsider, they must have appeared like a regular family—mum, dad, child. Whilst part of her relished the idea she knew it was dangerous to think of them that way. She and Marco *might* be Lily's parents but there was nothing binding them beyond that fact. Marco could disappear from their lives as swiftly as he had come, and she had to be prepared for that.

By the time she went into work, she was worn

out from worrying about it all. She was on late that day and AAU was buzzing when she arrived. Sister Thomas did the hand-over, sighing in relief after she finished.

'Am I glad to be going home. It's always busy in here but the problem about finding beds has made it worse than ever.'

'What's the latest on the ceiling?' Gina asked. 'Do they know how long it will take to repair it?'

'From what I can gather there may be a problem with the actual roof. They've called in a team of structural engineers to check it.' Eileen Thomas grimaced as she picked up her bag. 'If it ends up that we need a new roof, heaven only knows how long it's going to take.'

Gina sighed as Eileen departed. If a new roof was needed then the staff in AAU could find themselves under extra pressure for months to come.

There was no time to dwell on that thought, however. A patient had been referred to them by his GP after complaining of severe stomach cramps. His name was Adam Sanderson,

twenty-eight years old, and a painter and dec-
orator by trade. She got him settled then asked
Rosie which of the registrars was working that
evening. Typically, it was Miles, so she had him
paged then made a start on Adam's case history.
According to what he told her, he had never had
a day off sick until that week.

'Apart from the cramps, what other symptoms
have you had?' she asked, noting everything
down on the admission form.

'I've been sick a couple of times and I've had
the runs, too,' he told her, looking embarrassed.
'My girlfriend said it was probably the curry we
had the other night but I can't see it was that. I
mean, I've had a dodgy curry before but I've
never felt this rough!'

He groaned as he clutched his stomach. Gina
smiled sympathetically. 'We'll give you something for the pain once the doctor has seen you…
Here he is now, in fact.'

She stood up as Miles came striding down the
ward. He didn't bother to greet her but just held
out his hand for the notes. Gina bit her tongue

to hold back the reprimand as she handed them to him. Why did Miles have to make such an issue out of the fact that she had refused to go out with him?

'I've seen junior nurses make a better job of taking a case history,' he said witheringly, studying what she had written.

Gina forbore to say anything, refusing to justify herself by explaining that she hadn't had time to take a detailed history yet. She waited while he examined Adam, palpating his abdomen and asking a series of questions. She could tell from the look on Miles's face after he had finished that he hadn't a clue what was wrong with the other man, although that didn't deter him. One thing Miles didn't lack was confidence in his own ability.

'I need bloods and a urine test too.' He made a note on the file then turned to leave but she stopped him.

'Mr Sanderson is in a lot of discomfort from the stomach cramps.'

'Five milligrams of morphine.' Miles barely glanced at her as he wrote out the instruction and signed it. 'Call me as soon as the bloods come back, if you can remember to do that, Sister.'

It was insulting to suggest she would forget. However, there was no way that she was prepared to get into an argument with him in front of a patient. 'Of course,' she said coldly, her tone making it clear how annoyed she felt.

Adam grimaced as Miles strode away. 'What's up with him? He did nothing but have a go at you from the time he arrived.'

'Probably had a bad day,' she said lightly, although the time was fast approaching when she would have to do something about Miles's attitude towards her. She couldn't allow him to carry on trying to undermine her in front of their patients.

Adam sighed. 'Tell me about it.'

Gina went to fetch the morphine, wondering how best to deal with the problem of Miles. Normally, the logical step would be to have it out with him, but she had a feeling that was what Miles was hoping for. He was spoiling for a row and the last thing she wanted was for it to develop into a full-scale war.

Maybe she should have a word with Marco and ask him to intervene, she thought as she unlocked the drugs cupboard. And maybe she wouldn't, she decided. Involving Marco in her affairs was something she was trying to avoid. Lily was the only link between them and she must never forget that.

Marco could feel his stomach churning as he entered AAU. Gina was working the late shift and he had to admit that he was looking forward to seeing her. It seemed ages since Saturday and he had missed her.

The thought brought him to a halt. He had missed Gina and there was no point denying it. It was as though those few hours they had spent together in the park had awoken all the old feelings he had tried so hard to banish. He'd been on the brink of falling in love with her three years ago; was he right back where he had been then?

The thought was too much to deal with. Marco

drove it from his mind as he opened the office door. The room was empty so he headed into the ward, frowning when he failed to catch sight of her. When he spotted Julie, he called her over.

'Where's Gina? I thought she was working late today.'

'She is, although I'm not sure where she's gone, probably blowing off steam after her latest run-in with Miles.'

'What do you mean?' Marco demanded.

'Oh, nothing. I shouldn't have said anything.'

Julie hastily excused herself, but Marco had no intention of letting the matter drop. If there was a problem with his staff then he needed to know, especially if Gina was involved. He went back to the office and waited for her to arrive, which she did a few minutes later. He could tell at once that she was upset and was surprised by how protective he felt. If someone had upset her, they would have him to answer to!

'What is all this about you and Miles arguing?' he demanded, getting straight to the point.

She stopped dead when she saw him and he

could tell that she was loath to explain what had been going on. However, there was no way that he was prepared to overlook what had been happening.

'Is there a problem about you and Miles working together?'

'Er...no. Of course not.' She picked up a lab report off the desk and turned to leave.

'And you are sure about that, Gina?'

'Of course I am.' She gave him a tight smile. 'I need to phone Miles and let him know the blood results are back for this patient.'

She hurried out of the door although she could just as easily have made the call from there. Marco frowned as he watched her leave. He couldn't force her to tell him what was wrong, but he hoped she would confide in him. If something was worrying her, he wanted to help. Maybe they could never be together as a couple but he cared about what happened to her.

He took a deep breath as the thought expanded. He cared about her far more than he wanted to and far more than he should.

CHAPTER FOURTEEN

GINA left a message on Miles's phone to tell him that Adam Sanderson's blood results were back then helped Julie do the obs. With patients coming and going at various times of the day and night, it was something that needed to be kept track of on an individual basis. Two patients were down for fifteen-minute obs, so they did them first then did the rest. They had just finished when Miles came storming into the unit and headed straight over to her.

'I thought I asked you to let me know as soon as Mr Sanderson's bloods came back, Sister Lee.'

'You did. I left a message on your phone about an hour ago,' she replied, determined to keep her cool.

'Really? Funny that I don't seem to have received it, isn't it?'

His tone was sceptical and she bristled. 'If you're insinuating that I am lying then you can stop right there. I tried your phone. It was engaged so I left a message. End of story.'

'Well, we only have your word for it, don't we? If you want my opinion, I'd say you're covering your back because once again you failed to do what you were supposed to do.'

His tone was harsh and Gina shivered. This had gone past the stage of sour grapes. Miles was turning this into a vendetta and if something wasn't done to stop him, heaven knew what would happen next. She drew him aside.

'I don't take kindly to being spoken to that way, Dr Humphreys, especially when there is no justification for it.' She stared into his angry eyes. 'This has all to do with the fact that I refused to go out with you, hasn't it? I'm sorry if I hurt your feelings but it wasn't personal. I don't date because I have neither the time nor the inclination for a relationship.'

'Is everything all right?'

Gina spun round, feeling the colour run up

her cheeks when she discovered that Marco was standing behind her. It was obvious that he had heard what she'd said and she was mortified. Did she really want him to know that she had avoided emotional entanglements since they had parted?

'Everything is fine, isn't that so, Dr Humphreys?' She turned to Miles, the look she gave him challenging him to disagree.

'I...um...yes. If you'll excuse me.' Miles hurried away, obviously not wanting to continue the discussion in front of his boss either.

Marco frowned as he watched him leave. 'If Dr Humphreys is causing you a problem, Gina, I need to know.'

'It's a personal matter.' She turned to leave but he laid his hand on her arm.

'He is annoyed because you refused to go out with him?'

So he had overheard their conversation? Gina sighed. 'He asked me out a couple of months ago and won't accept that I'm not interested. I'm sure he'll get over it in time.'

'But in the interim he is making life difficult for you?'

She shrugged, neither agreeing nor disagreeing with the suggestion. Maybe Marco thought he was helping but she really and truly didn't want him involved in her affairs.

'Whilst I admire your discretion, Gina, I shall take a very dim view if the situation continues.' His tone was hard. 'If you two are at odds, it is going to affect the running of the department. I want this sorted out sooner rather than later. If you cannot resolve it yourself then I shall.'

He didn't give her a chance to reply as he walked away. Gina shook her head, feeling very much as though she had been run over by a steamroller. How dared he issue orders to her about her personal life?

She was about to follow him and tell him that in no uncertain terms only just at that moment Julie came hurrying over. A patient with suspected angina was experiencing chest pains again. Gina went to check on her and decided they needed the cardiothoracic reg. She asked Julie to have him paged then set about making the woman comfortable. By the time the registrar arrived and decided that an immediate bypass was necessary, there was no sign of Marco. It was after seven and no doubt he had gone home so she would need to have a word with him again.

She sighed as she headed for the canteen for her break. Marco might think he was helping but she didn't want him fighting her battles for her. She couldn't afford to rely on him when in a few months' time he would probably disappear from her life.

Marco couldn't believe how angry he felt. He'd had the overwhelming urge to punch Miles Humphreys on the nose when he had heard what he had said to Gina. He went into the consultants' lounge, intending to catch up on some of the more urgent paperwork, but he couldn't concentrate. So Gina wasn't interested in dating? She had turned down Miles's invitation but had she turned down many others too?

He frowned, wondering why the thought gave

him such a buzz. It was nothing to do with him what she did and yet the thought of her going out with another man was anathema to him. He would be more than happy if she refused every single invitation that came her way!

There was no chance of him settling down to work while that thought ran riot. He made his way to the canteen in the hope that a cup of coffee would clear his head. He used the stairs, bypassing the fourth floor where all the damage had been caused. The corridor had been roped off and there were warning signs advising people to keep out. The hospital had been extended over the years with this new section housing Women's Surgical and Paediatrics. It meant that the damaged part of the building could be isolated from the rest.

The canteen was empty when Marco arrived. He bought a cup of indifferent coffee from the machine and took it over to a table by the window. From there, he could see London spread out below. It was raining again, a thin grey drizzle that leached the light from the sky, and all of a sudden he was overwhelmed with homesickness.

What was he doing here when he could be in Florence? He had filled in the gaps in his memory, discovered he had a child and met her, too. No one would blame him if at the end of his tenure he returned home...

The door opened and he froze when he saw Gina come in. No one apart from Gina, that was. She would blame him for doing exactly what she had foretold. He had let her down and she was only waiting for him to do the same to Lily. His head began to spin as the enormity of what was happening struck him. He couldn't leave, not now, not in six months' time. He wanted to be part of his daughter's life forever and it meant that, by default, he would be part of Gina's too. And it was that last thought which filled him with a mixture of excitement and dread.

He was no longer in control of his life. He was being swept along by a tide too strong for him to fight.

Gina bought herself a cup of tea then looked for

somewhere to sit. The canteen was almost empty so she had plenty of choice but she paused when she saw Marco sitting by the window. There was no reason why she should join him and yet it seemed churlish to ignore him. She carried her cup across the room and stopped beside his table.

'Mind if I join you?'

'Please do.'

He stood up and politely pulled out a chair so she could sit down. He had always had exquisite manners, she thought as she got herself settled. It was one of the things she had loved about him, the fact that he had made her feel so special when they were out together—opening doors for her, handing her into the car, treating her in a way she had never been treated before.

The thought wasn't one she wanted to dwell on and she hurriedly took out a packet of sandwiches from her bag. 'I thought you'd have gone home by now,' she said, deeming it safer to make conversation than allow her mind to run off at tangents.

'I was intending to catch up on some paperwork but it held no appeal.' He gave her a wry smile. 'Paperwork was the bane of my life when I was a junior doctor and it hasn't improved with age.'

'You could get one of the registrars to do it. That's what our last consultant did. He never wrote any notes himself.'

'So I believe.' His tone was dry. 'Maybe it would have been better if he had. There would have been less…confusion.'

Gina laughed wryly. 'True.' She offered him the packet. 'Would you like a sandwich?'

'Thank you but no. I shall make myself a meal when I get in.' He sat back in his chair. 'So who looks after Lily when you work late?'

'My childminder.' She saw his brows rise and explained. 'Amy was a nurse before she had her own family so she understands the problems of doing shift work. She baths Lily and pops her into her pyjamas so I can put her straight to bed when we get home.'

'It can't be easy balancing childcare and work.'

'It's a juggle, as any working mum will tell you, but we manage,' she said a shade defensively.

'I'm sure you do. It's obvious that Lily is a very happy and contented little girl.'

Gina smiled. 'She is.'

'Do you have any family who help you?'

'No. My mum died when I was fifteen and dad remarried a few years later while I was at university. He and his new wife moved to New Zealand so I see very little of him these days.'

'No sisters, brothers, aunts, cousins, etcetera?'

'No, just me, but that's fine. I have Lily and I don't need anyone else.'

'Not even a partner?'

Gina shrugged. 'I don't have time for a relationship. I'm too busy working and looking after Lily.'

'Which is why you turned down Miles's invitation?'

'I wouldn't have gone out with him even if I'd been looking for romance, which I'm not.'

'He's not your type?'

'No, not that I have a type, as you put it.' Gina

broke the crust off the bread, hoping he wouldn't pursue the subject. What would she say if he asked her what sort of man she was attracted to?

'How about you?' she said quickly, terrified that she would say something stupid. Admitting that she wasn't interested in any man after going out with him would be a mistake.

'My parents are both dead and I, too, am an only child. Oh, there are lots of aunts and cousins but I see very little of them.' He shrugged. 'It isn't deliberate. We all lead busy lives and it's hard to find the time to meet. The only person I see regularly is Nonna—my maternal grandmother. She's very frail and a little confused these days, so she lives in a nursing home on the outskirts of Florence.'

'And there's no one special in your life?' she asked, then could have bitten her tongue because it was the last thing she should have asked him.

'No one at all.' He glanced down at his cup and his eyes were very dark when he looked up again, so dark that it was impossible to tell what he was thinking. 'Apart from Lily, of course.'

Gina knew she should be relieved to hear him state once again his interest in their daughter and she was. However, she couldn't ignore the disappointment she felt that he hadn't added her to his list of special people. She cleared her throat, knowing how stupid she was being. 'I'm glad to hear it. I get the impression she thinks you are pretty special too.'

He smiled at that. 'I hope so. I hope that given time she will come to love me as much as I love her.'

'Love? Surely it's a bit premature to claim that you love her, Marco?'

'Not at all. The moment I set eyes on her my heart was filled with love.' He paused, seemingly loath to continue, before suddenly carrying on. 'Sometimes it happens that way, Gina. You realise that you love someone even though it's against your better judgement.'

'Has it happened to you before?' she whispered, her heart pounding.

'*Si.*'

'With Francesca?'

'No. Francesca and I knew each other when we were children. Our love grew over the years.' He reached across the table and touched her hand. 'It was different when I met you. I knew that I would fall in love with you if I let myself.'

'And it wasn't what you wanted?'

'No. I didn't want it to happen then and I don't want it to happen now.'

'So you've given up on love altogether?'

'It is safer this way. I couldn't go through the kind of pain I went through when Francesca died. It's better to be alone than risk that happening.'

Gina felt her eyes swim with tears at the bleakness of that statement. It seemed wrong that Marco should deny himself the chance of finding happiness again. Even though she wasn't looking for romance either, she hadn't ruled it out, especially if there was a chance that Marco might change his mind.

The thought made her see how precarious her position was. She knew that Marco didn't want to pick up where they had left off—he had been quite blunt about that! However, even knowing that didn't stop her wishing for the impossible, the happy ending she had been denied three years ago.

'I am sorry, Gina. I did not mean to upset you. You have a tender heart.' He stroked her hand, making her shiver when she felt the faintly abrasive touch of his thumb caressing her skin, and she hurriedly withdrew her hand.

'My mother always said I was a softie.' She summoned a smile, ignoring the tremor that ran through her. She couldn't afford to be so vulnerable around him. 'I would cry at the least little thing—a sad film on television, something I'd read in the newspaper—you name it.'

'As I said, you have a tender heart.'

He gave her a tight smile. Gina frowned when she realised that he looked upset. 'Is something wrong?'

'Of course not.' He pushed back his chair. 'I shall have to make a start on that paperwork. *Ciao*, Gina. I hope the rest of the evening isn't too busy.'

He strode towards the door, not looking back

as he left. Gina picked up her sandwich, wondering what had caused him to react that way. Had it been it something she'd said, but what?

She racked her brain but couldn't come up with an answer. Maybe Marco had remembered something, something to do with Francesca, and that was what had caused him to look so bleak for a moment. It must be very difficult for him to have to relive the past as he must have done when he'd recovered his memory. Losing the woman he had loved had obviously devastated his life. Although he claimed that he'd been on the brink of falling in love with *her*, it wasn't the same, was it? He had been able to stop himself taking that final step and he couldn't have done that if he had felt for her even a fraction of what he had felt for his wife.

Gina got up and threw the rest of her sandwiches in the bin. The fact had to be faced: even if Marco hadn't split up with her, she would only ever have been second best.

CHAPTER FIFTEEN

THE next few weeks flew past. As Marco settled into his job, he found to his surprise that he was enjoying it. Although the hospital wasn't as well equipped as the ones he had worked in recently, the calibre of the staff made up for it. He refused to dwell on the thought that it was working with Gina that was the best thing of all, however. There was no point getting fixated on that idea.

They spent several more days at the park and each time Lily seemed very receptive to him. She was a naturally sunny-natured child and Marco was enchanted by her. Although he'd had little contact with any children beyond work, he seemed to know instinctively how to relate to her and that gave him confidence.

The fact that Gina gave him a free hand also helped. She seemed to trust him to know how high to push Lily on the swing or to assess the risks of allowing her to climb unaided up the slide, and he appreciated that. However, if he did defer to her, she never made him feel lacking in any way. It was obvious that she was doing all she could to make the situation easy for them, or rather easy for *Lily*. He must never forget that Lily was her main concern.

That thought caused him more than one pang of regret, akin to how he had felt when she had confessed that she had always been soft-hearted. Although he called himself every kind of a fool, he wished that her tears that night had been for *him* and not just because of what he had told her. He knew it wasn't fair to want her to engage her emotions when he couldn't return them, but working together made it extremely difficult to distance himself. She was in his thoughts from the moment he got up to the time he went to bed, and beyond, as the erotic dreams he had about her each night would testify. His mind might want to reject her but his body had very different ideas!

They had arranged to meet on Sunday that

week for either another trip to the park or to a local play centre if it was raining, so Marco was surprised when the phone rang just after eight on the Saturday night and discovered it was Gina. She got straight to the point.

'I'm afraid I'm going to have to cancel tomorrow's outing. Lily has chickenpox.'

'Oh, no!' he exclaimed, genuinely distressed by the thought. 'Is she very poorly?'

'She's hot and a bit fretful. I've given her liquid paracetamol for the temperature but I could really do with something to put on the spots to stop them itching.' She sighed. 'I've just got her settled, though, and I don't want to drag her out to the all-night chemist.'

'Certainly not. I shall get what you need and bring it round for you.'

'Oh, but I can't expect you to come all the way out here at this time of the night,' she protested.

'Why not?' Marco stamped down on a small spurt of irritation. 'I am her father and I want to be involved, Gina. That means helping during the bad times as well as during the fun ones.'

There was a small pause while she considered that. 'Well, in that case thank you.'

She gave him a list of what she needed and hung up. Marco fetched his jacket and set off. There was an all-night pharmacy close by so he went there first and then, on impulse, popped into the supermarket and bought a Chinese meal for two that only needed heating in the micro-wave. No doubt Gina had been too busy since she had got in from work and hadn't had time to eat anything.

He took a taxi to her home, grimacing as he got out of the cab. It certainly wasn't the best of locations, but at least it seemed to be relatively quiet. He made his way down the basement steps and knocked on the door, smiling when Gina opened it. 'The cavalry has arrived. Here you are.'

He handed her the pharmacy bag, carrying the one from the supermarket inside and placing it on the table. Although the flat looked bright and cheerful, it seemed incredibly small for two peo-ple, to his mind, although he didn't say so. Gina didn't need him criticising her home when she had a sick child to care for. However, it made him realise that he needed to do something about the situation. If Gina would allow him, of course.

'I'll just go and check on Lily. I may be able to dab some of this calamine on the spots if I'm careful.'

Gina headed towards what was evidently the bedroom and he followed, pausing in the doorway because there didn't seem to be room for him as well in the confined space. One corner had been partitioned off to form a minute second bedroom and he could see Lily tucked up in a child-sized bed. A toy box, some colourful cartoon prints on the wall and a small chest of drawers comprised the rest of the furnishings, and he was suddenly assailed by guilt. There he was living in that huge apartment all by himself while Gina and Lily were crammed into here!

'There isn't much room,' he said, unable to hold back the comment any longer.

'It's fine,' Gina assured him, tipping some calamine onto a pad of cotton wool. She gently dabbed it on Lily's face, murmuring soothingly when the little girl started to whimper. She dabbed at another couple of spots then grimaced. 'I'd better not risk doing any more. I'll wait until she wakes up. It should have helped, though. Thank you for bringing it over.'

It was obviously a hint that he should leave but he had no intention of going anywhere. How could he leave her to cope with a sick child on her own? 'There's some antihistamine syrup in the bag too—that will help control the itching.'

'Oh, right. Thank you.' She took out the package. 'Amy used that for the twins when they had it. It really helped.'

'Is that where Lily caught it, from the childminder's children?'

'I assume so.' She shrugged. 'By the time the twins' spots appeared Lily would have been infected so there was nothing I could do to prevent her getting it.'

'Better that she has it now rather than later.'

'Exactly.' She suddenly yawned and clapped her hand over her mouth. 'Oh, excuse me!'

'You're tired. You worked all day and I doubt if you've had any rest since you got in.'

'Lily has been a lot more demanding than normal,' she admitted, trying, unsuccessfully, to swallow another massive yawn. 'What I wouldn't give for a nice hot soak in the bath. It would wash away some of the cobwebs.'

'Then go and have one while Lily is asleep.'

'Oh, but I couldn't. I need to keep an eye on her…'

'Nonsense.' He placed his hands on her shoulders and propelled her towards the door of the miniscule bathroom, trying not to think about the state-of-the-art facilities back at his apartment. 'I shall look after Lily. You need some time for yourself, Gina. It could be a long night.'

'I don't expect you to look after her, Marco! She's my child, after all.'

'No, she is *our* child and that makes her my responsibility as well.' He gave her a gentle push, wondering when she would accept that his interest wasn't a passing thing. He was in it for the long haul and to his mind that meant for ever. He made his voice sound as reassuring as possible. 'I shall take good care of her, Gina. Trust me.'

Gina hesitated, not sure that she liked being told what to do. However, she had to admit that a bath could make the world if difference if she had to get up during the night.

'If you're sure,' she began, then tailed off when Marco's brows lifted in that deliciously sexy way that always made her insides feel as though they were melting into puddles of hot liquid. Swinging round, she hurried into the bathroom and locked the door, leaning back against it while she caught her breath. Stop it! she told herself sternly. This isn't the time to be having such lascivious thoughts.

Turning on the water, she filled the bath, adding a generous dollop of bubble bath so that foam frothed over the side as she slid into the water. She sighed luxuriously as she closed her eyes and let the heat soak into her tired limbs. She had no idea what Marco was doing because she couldn't hear a sound coming from the living room, and she didn't care. Maybe he was sitting quietly on the couch, waiting for her to finish.

The thought triggered another, far more erotic one. Gina bit her lip as she recalled the times she had come out of the bathroom at his villa to find him lying on the bed, waiting for her. He wouldn't say a word but would simply hold out his hand. Words hadn't been necessary. They had each known what would happen next, how he would pull her down beside him and strip off her damp towel. His eyes would travel the length of her body, drinking in each curve, each dip, each hollow, and if he had found any imperfections, he certainly hadn't let her see that. When his eyes had come back to hers they had been filled with desire, with need.

Gina groaned softly, recalling how sweet their lovemaking had been. Marco had been a wonderfully generous lover, taking care to ensure she had enjoyed it as much as he had done, and she had. He had raised her to heights she had never experienced before, made her feel things she had never felt for any man apart from him; made her feel things she would never feel again because it was only in his arms that she became truly alive.

Her heart caught painfully as she was forced to face the truth. It was only when she was with Marco that she understood how it really felt to be a woman.

A soft tap at the door broke the spell. Gina opened her eyes, feeling an aching sense of loss seeping deep into her bones. No matter who came into her life in the future, she would never feel for him what she'd felt for Marco. 'Yes? Is it Lily? Is she all right?'

'She's fast asleep. I just wanted to know if you had eaten since you got home.'

'No. I haven't had time,' she told him, struggling to contain her emotions. She couldn't afford to indulge herself like this when it would make the situation all the more stressful. So far she and Marco had coped extremely well and the last thing she wanted was to ruin things. 'I'll get something later.'

'There is no need. I have brought some food with me. Ten minutes and it will be ready. *Si?*'

He obviously didn't expect a reply and she didn't give him one. She heard him walk towards the kitchen and a moment later heard the microwave ping open. Pulling the plug out of the bath, she wrapped a towel around her, wishing she had something more substantial to cover herself with as she hurried the short distance to the bedroom. There was a little too much bare thigh on show for comfort, not that Marco seemed upset by it when he glanced round, a small voice pointed out. In fact, he had looked rather interested.

Gina's teeth snapped together. Marco wasn't *interested*! She was just being silly.

Marco put the containers into the microwave then had to pause before he set the timer. He breathed in deeply, but the sight of Gina in that towel had had an unnerving effect. He closed his eyes but that only made matters worse. Now all he could see was the smooth, pale skin of her shoulders, her shapely thighs, the curve of her breasts thrusting against the damp fabric...

He swore under his breath and stabbed at the buttons on the microwave. He had to stop this. It was one thing to indulge his fantasies when he was alone in bed, but it was entirely different to do so here in Gina's home. She would be horrified if she had any idea what he was thinking!

By the time she appeared dressed in an all-concealing navy tracksuit, he had himself in hand. He turned when he heard her footsteps, battening down the fleeting thought that he much preferred her previous outfit. 'Good timing. This is just about ready. All I need now are plates and cutlery.'

'I'll get them.'

She inched past him to reach into the cupboard above the stove and he sucked in his breath when he felt her breasts brush his shoulder. He could tell from the brief contact that she wasn't wearing a bra and it was just the sort of thought his body needed to run riot again. Stepping back, he attempted to give her some room but the damage had been done. Every nerve now was on high alert, so that when she stood on tiptoe to reach the top shelf, causing the muscles in her shapely backside to tauten, he almost groaned out loud.

How was he going to keep his hands to himself if he had to face this kind of temptation?

'Got them.' Gina smiled as she turned round. 'We'll use the good plates instead of the ones Lily and I usually use.' She placed a couple of china plates on the counter and turned back to the cupboard. 'I just need a couple of glasses now.'

'Let me get them for you,' Marco said hastily, unable to withstand much more. He took a couple of glasses off the shelf and placed them on the counter. 'Is that everything?'

'Apart from the cutlery. It's in the drawer under the sink.'

She went to get it but he shook his head. Opening the drawer, he took out the cutlery and handed it to her. 'I'll serve the food if you would lay the table.'

'Of course.'

She shot him a puzzled look as she headed towards the window where a small table had been placed in the bay. Marco's mouth tightened as he lifted the hot dishes out of the microwave. Had she sensed something was amiss? He hoped not but if she had then he would do his best to set her mind at rest. The last thing he wanted was for her to think he was coming onto her!

By the time he took the plates over to the table, he felt more in control. Gina looked up when he placed a plate in front of her and smiled. 'That smells delicious. What is it?'

'Chicken Foo Yung is what it said on the carton.' He went back for the wine and unscrewed the top of the bottle. 'I'm not sure if this goes with it or not, but we can only try.'

He reached over to fill her glass but she stopped him. 'I'm not sure if I should. Lily could wake up and I don't want to risk not hearing her.'

'Half a glass should be fine, surely,' he said quietly, leaving the final decision to her.

'All right, then. Just half a glass.'

Marco poured her some wine then poured some for himself. Lifting the glass to his lips, he took a sip. 'It's not great, but not as bad as I feared.'

She took a small swallow of the pale liquid. 'It tastes fine to me but then I'm not exactly a connoisseur. I can't even remember the last time I had a glass of wine with my meal.'

She took another sip then picked up her fork, obviously relishing the simple meal. Unlike so many women, she didn't toy with her food: she enjoyed it. He had always found the way she had savoured all the new tastes he had introduced her to incredibly sexy, in fact, and it was just as erotically stimulating now, he realised.

Marco forked up a mouthful of chicken, trying to keep his mind from setting off down that track. He was here to help her and he must remember that. They ate in silence for several minutes before she gave a small sigh.

'This is a real treat. Just being able to sit here and enjoy the food is such a lovely change. Don't get me wrong—Lily is very good—but it's usually a question of grabbing a mouthful in between helping her. Thank you, Marco, for thinking of it.'

'It is my pleasure, *cara*.' The endearment slid out before he thought about it and he felt heat invade him when he saw her stiffen. It had felt as natural as breathing to call her that and it wasn't the most settling of thoughts in the circumstances.

They finished their meal, making desultory conversation, mainly, he suspected, because she felt uncomfortable with the silence. Was she recalling other meals they had shared when the food had been merely a precursor to a whole lot more?

He longed to know the answer and yet at the same time feared it. To know that she was as aware of him as he was of her would be too difficult to deal with. The trouble was that his mind wanted him to remain detached while the rest of him wanted the exact opposite.

It made him wonder which part would win. Would he be able to conquer this attraction he felt for her or would he be forced to give in? And if he did, where would it end? He may have been able to stop himself falling in love with her three years ago but he knew in his heart that he wouldn't be able to stop it now.

He took a deep breath. If he gave in, there would be absolutely nothing he could do to save himself.

CHAPTER SIXTEEN

GINA wasn't sure if the tension was all in her mind. On the surface, Marco seemed to be behaving as he normally did as they discussed a range of topics mainly centred on work. So why did she have the feeling that his thoughts were a long way away from the vagaries of the National Health Service?

She stood up abruptly, refusing to create problems where none might exist. 'How about coffee? I don't know about you but I could do with a cup.'

'Thank you, that would be nice.'

His tone was as bland as the smile he gave her. Gina knew she should have been reassured yet she wasn't. Marco was masking his feelings, deliberately hiding them from her, and the thought was more disturbing than it should be. Picking up their plates, she took them to the sink then filled the kettle, wondering how soon she could bring the evening to a close. As soon as they had drunk their coffee, she decided, she would make it clear that she expected him to leave.

She made the coffee and placed the cafetière on the table in front of the couch. 'We may as well sit here to drink it. It's more comfortable than those hard chairs.'

Marco walked over to the couch and sat down, leaving her to either sit next to him or perch on the stool. She opted for the stool, preferring the discomfort to sitting beside him. The couch wasn't very large and each time they moved, their arms would touch. A shiver ran through her and she hurriedly busied herself with serving the coffee.

'I hope this is all right for you,' she said, handing him a cup. 'It's only the supermarket's own brand, I'm afraid.'

'After the stuff that comes out of that machine in the canteen, it will taste like nectar,' he observed wryly.

Gina laughed, relieved to be distracted from her

unruly thoughts. 'It *is* awful, isn't it? Everyone has complained but the management claim it's less expensive to use a machine than employ someone to make tea and coffee.'

'They haven't factored in staff morale, obviously.' He laughed deeply. 'There would be far fewer absences if there was some decent coffee available.'

'Probably,' she agreed, trying to control the sudden fluttering in her stomach. How she wished she wasn't so aware of him that even the sound of his laughter immediately drew a response from her. She stood up abruptly, needing a moment's respite from the torment. 'I'd better check on Lily again.'

The little girl was fast asleep. Gina smoothed back her hair and straightened the quilt but that took only a moment and she needed more time to collect herself. She glanced round when she heard a sound behind her, feeling the fluttering intensify when she realised that Marco had followed her. In the dim glow from the nightlight he looked so big and vitally male that she couldn't fail to be aroused and it was the last thing she needed. It took her all her time to remain where she was as he came over to the bed.

'How is she?' He laid a gentle hand on Lily's forehead and frowned. 'She feels rather hot.'

'The paracetamol liquid I gave her earlier should bring her temperature down,' she assured him.

'Of course it will. *Mi scusi.* I did not mean to imply that you were not looking after her properly, Gina.'

'I know you didn't.'

She eased past him, anxious to make some space between them. The close confines of the room were doing nothing to help the situation, she thought dizzily as she breathed in the scent of his aftershave, something spicy and wholly masculine that stirred her senses all the more. Her foot suddenly caught on the edge of the toy box and she cried out in alarm when she felt herself pitch forward.

'Careful!' All of a sudden Marco was there, his hand gripping her arm as he saved her from falling. He set her back on her feet then looked into her face. 'Are you all right? You have not hurt yourself?'

'No, I'm fine. I just tripped over the edge of the toy box,' she explained, her heart pounding although whether from the fall or his nearness she wasn't sure. She summoned a wobbly smile. 'I should look where I'm going.'

'There is not much room...' He shrugged eloquently, his broad shoulders rising beneath the thin silk shirt he was wearing.

Gina felt a frisson of raw need run through her when she felt the solid wall of his chest brush against her nipples. It wasn't intentional on his part; they were simply standing so close that the moment he moved, his body made contact with hers. However, the effect was just as devastating as if it had been planned.

'Gina.' Her name was part groan, part plea as it emerged from his throat. It touched a chord inside her, one that she might not have responded to otherwise. He sounded as though he, too, was fighting his feelings and she knew how that felt. She really did!

Her eyes lifted to his and she knew that she was right when she saw the expression they held. He was looking at her with such hunger that there could be no mistake about what he wanted. Marco wanted her. He wanted her as a man wanted a woman he found deeply attractive and all of a sudden she knew it was what she wanted too.

'Marco.'

She said his name, softly and without inflection, and saw his eyes darken as he realised what she was doing. This had to be a decision they both made; neither must coerce the other and then have regrets. When his hand lifted to her cheek, she stood quite still, feeling the faintly abrasive touch of his fingertips skimming the line of her jaw, the curve of her cheekbone, the fullness of her lips. She had the feeling that he was relearning the shape and feel of her all over again and knew that it was something he needed to do. He had forgotten such a lot; had he for-gotten this as well?

'Your skin is so soft,' he whispered, his fingers stroking and caressing her. 'I always thought it felt like velvet...'

He broke off, his hand stilling as the thought settled into his consciousness, another memory returned. When his fingers moved on, gliding down her throat, she could feel the tremor in them and knew that it had affected him deeply to realise that he had wanted her this much once before.

His hand slid down her throat until it came to the zip on her jacket and could go no further. Gina didn't move, leaving it to him to decide if he should go further. She knew what she wanted and he had to do the same.

His hand reached for the zip at last and she held her breath. She hadn't bothered with un-derwear after her bath and suddenly wished she had. When he started to run the zipper down its track, she bit her lip. It had been a long time since Marco had seen her naked and she'd had

Lily since. Her body had changed as a woman's body did after she'd borne a child.

'You are so beautiful, *cara*. So much a woman.'

His tone was hoarse and she shuddered when she heard the emotion it held. There wasn't a doubt in her mind that he was telling her the truth as he parted the edges of her jacket and looked at her. Maybe her body had changed but he liked what he saw, and that was all she had needed to know.

She lifted her face, letting him see what she wanted not with words but by expression, and heard him groan. Bending, he covered her mouth with his, his lips drawing a response from her that she was more than willing to give. The kiss ran on and on and Gina knew that he was as help-less as she was to stop it. They needed this kiss, needed to feast on each other's lips to slake just a bit of this hunger they both felt.

'Dio mio!' Marco drew back at last although he didn't let her go. Gina could feel the tremor that was running through his body, a wire-taut tension that was mirrored by the tension inside

her. Nobody could have kissed or been kissed like that without being stirred to the very depths of their soul.

'I didn't realise...'

He tailed off, either unable or unwilling to put his feelings into words, but he didn't need to. She understood how he felt because she felt the same. She always had done. Whenever Marco had kissed her, she had felt raw and shaken, alive in a way she had never been before. Had Marco felt that way three years ago or was this a new experience for him? She had no idea and wouldn't ask him either. Whichever answer he gave would only create problems.

Her heart lurched at the thought that maybe he was more attracted to her now than he had been in the past, but she refused to dwell on it. He had been unequivocal when he had told her that he would never get involved in a relationship again and it would be foolish to hope he might change his mind. She had to accept that this was all they had, this rawness of desire, this need that burned within them. It might not be what she had hoped for once but it was enough for now. It had to be.

She wound her arms around his neck and drew his head down so that she could kiss him. Marco had loved it when she had instigated their love-making in the past and it was obvious that he appreciated it now. His lips immediately parted, allowing her free licence as she deepened the kiss, her tongue sliding inside the warm, coffee-flavoured recesses of his mouth to mate with his. When he pulled her closer so that she could feel the rigid tautness of his erection pressing into her, she smiled. It was the response she had wanted, the one she had expected, too.

'So you think it is funny that I want you this much,' he said softly in her ear, his hips moving against hers so that she gasped.

'I think it's…sweet,' she said, struggling to control the rush of desire that shot through her.

'Sweet?' His tone said what he thought of that adjective and she laughed, loving the fact that she could make him rise with her teasing. *'Sweet!'*

'Hmm. I mean, I think it's really nice that you're so keen...'

She didn't get the chance to finish as he swung her up into his arms and carried her into the living room. He deposited her on the couch and smiled wolfishly at her. 'Oh, I am keen, *tesoro*. I think you can take that as read.'

He knelt beside her, parting the front of her jacket so that he could stroke her breasts. Gina shivered when she felt the pads of his thumbs edging ever closer to her nipples. She could feel them peaking in anticipation but each time she thought he would touch her there, his hands moved away, his thumbs tracing lazy circles on her skin until she felt she would explode with need.

'Marco, please,' she murmured, arching her back.

'Please what, my darling? Please stop? Please continue? Just tell me what it is you want and I shall do my best to oblige like the *sweet* man I am.'

Gina knew he was teasing her and it was a revelation. Although they'd had fun together in the past, making love had been a far more serious business. Marco hadn't teased her like this then and it was oddly disturbing to be on the receiving end of it now. She frowned, unsure what to make of this new side of him, and he paused.

'What is it, Gina? Is something wrong?'

'No...well, I'm not sure.' She bit her lip, uncertain if she should say anything.

'Tell me.' He bent and kissed her on the mouth, a kiss that was filled with reassurance. 'I don't want there to be any more secrets between us.'

She knew it was a gentle reminder of the biggest secret that she had kept from him—Lily— and flushed. 'There won't be. It's just that when we were together three years ago, you were different, Marco, less...playful.'

'Si?' He frowned this time. 'You mean when we made love?'

'Exactly. You never teased me like this. You were far more serious...' She broke off and shrugged. 'It was just different.'

'Maybe because I was different.' He cupped her

cheek and his expression was grave. 'I felt guilty about wanting another woman, Gina, so maybe that was why making love to you was such a serious matter.'

'And you don't feel guilty now?' she whispered.

'No. Not that way at least.' He looked into her eyes. 'I shall feel incredibly guilty, though, if I cause you any distress, so think long and hard about what we are doing, *amata*. Is this what you really want when I can't make you any promises for the future?'

Marco held his breath as he waited for her answer. He wanted her so much that it hurt, wanted to bury himself inside her softness, feel himself enveloped by her sweetness, but if it wasn't what she truly wanted then he would stop. Maybe he shouldn't have allowed things to progress this far but he had and now he would have to deal with the consequences—whatever they were.

His heart lurched at the thought that there would be consequences from this night but before he could have second thoughts, Gina's hand lifted. She touched his face, her fingers brushing his cheek, and once again there was that flash of memory, the knowledge deep inside that she had done the same thing before.

'But I do want this, Marco. I want us to make love for many reasons. Maybe it will help to lay a few ghosts from the past. I'm not sure. But what I am sure about is that I want it to happen.'

It was the affirmation he needed and yet still he hesitated. She talked about laying ghosts but would it? Or would it merely create more problems, make it harder for them to be parents to Lily? They had coped so well these past weeks, worked in surprising harmony, but such a massive shift in their relationship could alter everything.

All of a sudden Marco didn't know which way to turn. He wanted her so much he ached. And yet making love with her could open the way to all sorts of complications he wasn't sure he could face. It would take so little, so very little, to fall in love with her and then what would he do? Even if she reciprocated his feelings—and there was no saying that she would after the way he had hurt her—could he imagine living on a knife-edge, always fearing that something dreadful would happen to ruin his happiness?

The old fears came rushing back and he knew that he couldn't do it. He couldn't take the risk of loving her and losing her—his heart wouldn't withstand that kind of grief again.

He drew back, knowing that once he made this decision he would have to stick to it. He couldn't toy with her emotions, couldn't blow hot one minute and cold the next, as she had put it. Either they moved their relationship forward and became lovers or they stayed as they were: Lily's parents and friends. Nothing more.

'I'm sorry, Gina,' he said, his voice sounding rough when it emerged from his throat. 'I should never have allowed the situation to reach this point.'

'It wasn't solely your decision, Marco.'

He winced when he heard the hurt in her voice even though she did her best to disguise it. The last thing he wanted was to hurt her and yet once again he had done so. 'No. It wasn't. And don't think I'm not flattered by the fact that you want me, Gina, because I am. It's more than I expected after the way I treated you and far more than I deserve. I just think it would be a mistake to… confuse the issue.'

'If that's how you feel, I'm sure you're right.'

She zipped up her jacket and Marco felt his heart ache at the finality of the action. Just for a second he was tempted to tell her he had changed his mind but he managed to bite back the words. He couldn't allow desire to rule his head as well as his heart.

The thought that his heart was already engaged was disturbing. He knew that he needed time to come to terms with what was happening. Maybe he'd been able to pull back from the brink of falling in love three years ago, but it would be far harder to do so now. Gina wasn't just the woman he wanted; she was the mother of his child. And that made her even more special in his eyes, even more desirable. He stood up abruptly. 'I'd better go.'

'Of course.' She followed his lead, masking her

feelings as she saw him to the door. 'Thank you for bringing those things for Lily. I appreciate it.'

'Don't mention it.' His tone was as polite as hers was, which was surprising bearing in mind that inside he was seething with frustration. How he wished he could think of something to say that would make them both feel better but the right words—if there were any *right* words in a situation like this—escaped him. All he could do was pretend that nothing had happened, that a few minutes ago they hadn't been on the verge of making love.

A spasm of need shot through his body and he reached blindly for the latch. 'I hope Lily doesn't keep you up all night,' he said thickly, glancing over his shoulder. Gina was standing behind him and for a second her expression was unguarded. His heart ached when he saw the pain in her eyes because he knew he was responsible for putting it there.

'We'll be fine.' She pinned a smile to her lips and the sheer bravery of the action touched him on many levels. 'Sleepless nights are par for the course when you're a mum.'

'I'm sure they are.' Marco longed to say that they should be par for the course when you were a father too but that would have been pushing things too far. He couldn't offer to stay and help her look after their daughter, not when he couldn't trust himself around her. He opened the door and then paused, needing a salve for his conscience. 'If there's anything else you need, just let me know and I'll bring it over.'

'Thank you but I have everything now.'

She started to close the door, making it clear that she wanted him to leave. Marco knew that he should go rather than prolong the agony and yet he found himself lingering.

'You will call me if there's a problem, won't you?'

'There won't be any problems, Marco. It's chickenpox, that's all. Lily will be right as rain in a few days' time.' She edged the door across and he knew that he couldn't drag it out any longer.

'*Bene.* I shall phone you in the morning to see how she is, if that is all right with you?'

'Of course.'

A last smile and then the door closed, leaving him on one side and her on the other. Marco sucked in a huge breath of cool night air, hoping it would help him put what had happened into some kind of perspective. As he walked up the basement steps, he ran back over everything that had happened since Gina had phoned him: his dash to the pharmacy; his insistence that she should have a bath; dinner; the near-fall in the bedroom.

It had been fine up till that point, a nice neat sequence of events that needed little explanation. However, what had happened after that was entirely different. Marco flagged down a passing taxi and gave the driver his address, his head feeling as though it would explode as he climbed into the back. There was nothing neat about his memories after that stumble. They were all jumbled up, a maelstrom of feelings and sensations: the softness of Gina's skin; the rounded firmness of her breasts; the heat inside him when he had pressed his body against hers.

He closed his eyes and let the erotic images seep deep into his consciousness. These were new memories, ones he wanted to store away so that he could retrieve them in the future when times were bleak. He knew how it felt to forget the important things and he didn't want to risk that happening again. If he couldn't have Gina then at the very least he could look back on this night and recall how good it had been to hold her in his arms and be held in hers. For those too-brief minutes he hadn't felt lonely. He had felt complete.

Gina managed to hold back her tears until the door closed but the moment the lock snapped shut they poured down her face. She went and sat down on the couch, thinking back over what had so nearly happened there. Marco had wanted her—she knew he had! However, his desire for her hadn't been enough in the end. Was it guilt that had stopped him making love to her, reluctance to betray the woman he had loved and lost?

It was the reason why he had ended their relationship before and it seemed the most likely explanation now. She knew she should accept that he would never get over Francesca, but she couldn't. The thought of him loving another woman to that extent was like having a knife plunged into her heart when she loved him so much.

She sat quite still as the thought settled deep into her mind. She loved Marco. Maybe it should have shocked her to face up to how she felt but it didn't. On some inner level she had been aware of her feelings for a while, but had not allowed herself to acknowledge them. Now it was a relief to face the truth.

She loved Marco and had never stopped loving him. Oh, she had been hurt and angry at the way he had treated her but not even that had been enough to destroy the love she felt for him. That was why she had been so eager to make love with him tonight. Not because she had wanted to lay some ghosts from the past but because she had wanted *him.*

Now she was ready to admit the truth, she could no longer pretend. She loved him with her whole heart and that made her vulnerable, but, worst of all, it made Lily vulnerable too. She couldn't allow herself to be ruled by her emotions where her precious child was concerned. She only needed to recall how swiftly Marco had changed his mind tonight to know how dangerous it would be.

She rubbed her hands over her face to wipe away her tears. Marco had wanted her tonight too, but he had changed his mind in the end. He couldn't be allowed to do the same to Lily.

CHAPTER SEVENTEEN

MARCO was aware that there had been a shift in Gina's attitude towards him. Although she was her usual courteous self in work, there was a new reserve about her. He knew what lay behind it and cursed himself for allowing his desire for her to get the better of him. The thought that he might have damaged their relationship was more than he could bear yet what could he do? If he apologised for almost making love to her, it could make the situation even worse.

It was all very frustrating and he found it difficult to put it out of his mind even while he was working. AAU was busier than ever, the ongoing repairs to the roof, causing everyone a headache. Patients were left on the unit long after they should have been moved to a ward. Consequently tempers became frayed as the staff dealt with the added pressure of overcrowding.

Marco tried to smooth things over as best he could, making endless phone calls to the various departments to chivvy them up. Although it wasn't his job, he found that if he phoned them personally there was a better chance of something being done. A request from the consultant carried more weight than a request from a member of the nursing staff.

He was about to make a couple more calls when he became aware of raised voices coming from the staffroom. It had been an exceptionally busy morning and he knew that everyone had been pushed way beyond their limits. He made a detour in that direction because the last thing they needed was the team at odds if they were to get through this stressful period. Pushing open the door, he came to a halt when he was confronted by the sight of Gina and Miles. It was immediately obvious they had been arguing.

'What's going on?' he demanded, looking from one to the other.

'Sister Lee was just trying to explain why she had failed to follow my instructions.' Miles turned to him. 'I specifically requested that a patient should be sent for a CT as soon as possible. However, Sister, in her infinite wisdom, decided it could wait. In the meantime, the patient suffered a bleed. It's in the lap of the gods now as to what happens but one thing is certain. If the patient dies, *she* is responsible!'

Miles pointed an accusing finger at Gina, who blanched. Marco came to a swift decision. 'I shall deal with this, Dr Humphreys. Can you bring me the patient's notes? I shall be in the office. Sister Lee, if you'd come with me, please.'

'I...um...the notes will have gone to Theatre,' Miles said hurriedly as Marco turned to leave, and he paused.

'In that case, please phone them and ask if we can borrow them. It shouldn't be a problem.'

Miles didn't look happy but quite frankly Marco didn't care. He led the way to the office with his heart sinking. It was a very serious accusation and could incur disciplinary charges if it was true. He sat down behind the desk and waved Gina towards the chair. 'I want to hear your version of what happened.'

She sat down and looked steadily back at him. 'My version? I don't have a version. All I can tell you is the truth. Dr Humphreys never requested that a CT scan should be done. His only instruction was that the patient should be placed on half-hourly obs.'

'Then why did he claim that he had requested a scan?' Marco queried.

'Probably because he knew he'd made a mistake and wanted to shift the blame away from himself,' she retorted. 'It's not the first time he's done that and it won't be the last, either.'

'I see. And is there anyone who can verify what you say?'

'No. The rest of the staff were attending to other patients. I was on my own, so it's my word against his.' She raised her chin. 'I am not lying. Miles never requested a CT scan.'

'Then it will show that in the patient's notes.' Marco looked up when Miles appeared. He held out his hand for the file, skimming through the notes which had been written since the woman had been admitted. He paused when he came to a section near the bottom of the page. 'It says here that you requested a CT scan at eleven-fifteen, Dr Humphreys. Is that correct?'

'Yes. It's written down there, plain to see.'

There was a triumphant note in Miles's voice that made Marco's hackles rise, although he didn't say anything. He read to the end of the report, which stated that the woman had been taken to Theatre to have a suspected subdural haematoma removed. 'Is there any news from Theatre?' he asked, glancing up.

'Not yet.' Miles sounded unbearably smug. 'However, I think those notes are conclusive, don't you? I did request a CT scan and Sister failed to carry out my instructions.'

'Thank you, Dr Humphreys.' Marco closed the file, refusing to be drawn into passing judgment even though it did appear as though Gina had made an error. 'That will be all for now. I shall speak to you later.' He waited until the younger man had left then handed her the file. 'Do you have anything to say about this, Gina?'

'No.' She stared at the notes in confusion. 'I don't know how that got there because the request certainly wasn't in the file before. Miles definitely didn't write it in these notes while I was with him.'

'You think he may have filled it in later, after he realised there was a problem with the patient?'

'I don't know... I mean, would he risk falsifying notes like that?' She looked up and he could see the worry in her eyes. 'All I know is that he never mentioned a scan to me.'

'I believe you, but I wish there was someone who could back up your story.' He shook his head. 'The fact that this instruction is in the file will carry a great deal of weight if it comes to a disciplinary hearing.'

'You think it could come to that?'

Marco sighed. 'If the patient doesn't pull through, then, yes, it could.'

'It would mean I'd get the blame.' She bit her

lip and he could tell how upset she was. 'Even though I swear it wasn't my fault.'

'It could do. We shall have to hope that it won't come to that, but you need to be aware that you're in a very difficult position, Gina.'

'And Miles will do all he can to make sure that he remains blameless,' she observed bitterly.

There was nothing Marco could say to dispute that. From what he had seen Miles would do anything he could to wriggle out of admitting his mistakes and if that meant ruining Gina's career, so be it. When she excused herself he didn't try to stop her. They would have to wait and see how the patient fared before further steps were taken. However, he knew that if he had to choose sides that he would choose Gina's.

She wouldn't lie about something like this. It wasn't in her nature. However, even his support would carry very little weight if it came to an inquiry and the facts were presented. The thought of her being subjected to that kind of ordeal was more than he could bear. He might not be able to commit himself to a relationship but it didn't

mean that he didn't care about her. On the con-
trary, he cared a lot. He cared so much that the
thought of her getting hurt, hurt him even more.

The next twenty-four hours were a nightmare.
The patient under question, Harriet Walters, was
moved to ICU and the prognosis wasn't good.
Gina tried not to let it worry her but it was impossible when Miles made a point of recounting
his version of events to anyone who would listen.
Whilst most believed she wasn't at fault, she was
realistic enough to know that some would accept
his story. When Harriet Walters died two days
later and her family demanded an inquiry, Gina
realised that she could be in a lot of trouble. The
thought that she might lose her job over this was
very hard to deal with. She had no idea how she
would support herself and Lily if that happened.

The thought was constantly on her mind so
that she found it difficult to sleep and woke each
morning exhausted. It didn't help that Lily was
still rather fretful thanks to the chickenpox. Gina
felt as though she was struggling to keep on top

of things and hated the fact that she seemed to have so little control over her life. However, when Marco offered to look after Lily to give her a break, she refused. Lily was her responsibility and it was up to her to look after her.

Marco had never felt so powerless in his life. He knew that Gina was worn out from trying to cope with Lily and the situation at work but she refused to let him help her. It made him see that whilst she might be willing to allow him access to Lily, she still didn't trust him. The fact that he hadn't helped his case the night they had almost made love was something he bitterly regretted. It would need drastic action to convince her that he was sincere about wanting to be a good father and there was just one way he could think of that might achieve that, even though he knew how risky it was.

He made arrangements to see Lily the following Saturday, determined that they were going to resolve the situation. It had been raining on and off all week so they met at a soft play centre in Camden. Marco was already there when

Gina arrived and he couldn't help thinking how lovely she looked in a pair of trim-fitting jeans and a pale blue T-shirt, with her blonde hair falling softly around her face.

He forced the thought aside as he bent down to lift Lily out of her pushchair. He couldn't afford to let his emotions run riot. If his plan was to succeed then he needed to remain in control. *'Buon giorno, cara,'* he said, trying to calm his wildly hammering heart as he kissed the little girl on the cheek and thought about what he intended to say to Gina.

'Buon giorno.' Lily smiled as she proudly repeated the phrase and he laughed.

'What a clever girl you are!' He gave her a hug then watched as she ran off to play in the ball pit. He turned to Gina, smoothing his face into a suitably noncommittal expression so that she couldn't tell how on edge he felt. 'She is starting to learn the odd Italian phrase, I see.'

'She is. Children pick things up so quickly at this age. They're like sponges,' she said quietly, lifting her bag out of the pushchair before parking it against the wall.

'So they say, although it's the first time I've actually witnessed it,' he replied lightly, pulling out a chair for her. 'Another plus of being a parent, wouldn't you agree?'

She shrugged as she sat down. 'To counteract the minuses, you mean?'

'No, that wasn't what I meant,' he replied in exasperation. 'Why do you always put such a negative slant on whatever I say, Gina? Can't you accept that I am thrilled about being a father?'

'Because I find it hard to believe that you won't grow tired of the responsibility that comes with the title. Anyone can claim to be a father, Marco, but it takes a lifetime of commitment to prove you can do the job.'

'And you don't think I can make such a long-term commitment?'

'No. If you want the truth , I don't.'

She stared coolly back at him but underneath the calm mask he could sense her fear and it touched him. All of a sudden he knew that he couldn't wait any longer. He couldn't bear to leave her worrying for a second longer than was necessary.

'Then maybe this will convince you.' Reaching out, he took hold of her hand. 'I want you to marry me, Gina.'

Just for a moment, Gina thought she must have misheard him. It was extremely noisy in the play centre with all the children running about after all. Her heart began to pound as she stared at him and read the expression on his face. It was true: Marco had asked her to marry him. It was what she had dreamed about three years ago, what she still wanted now, she realised with a sudden rush of joy. Marrying him, being with him, loving him and being loved by him was what she wanted more than anything!

She opened her mouth to tell him that, yes, she would marry him, that she could think of nothing she wanted more, when he carried on.

'It makes sense, doesn't it? If we get married then we'll be able to provide Lily with everything she needs.'

'You're asking me to marry you for Lily's sake?' she said hoarsely, feeling the pain scoring deep inside her. She didn't know why she should feel so hurt. Marco had made it clear many times that he wasn't interested in having a relation-ship with her, yet she had managed to forget that in the heat of the moment. The ache inside her seemed to intensify as he continued in the same pragmatic tone.

'Yes. If you marry me then you won't have to work—you can spend all your time with Lily. She'd also be able to live somewhere more suit-able. Your flat is far too small for a growing child. There's hardly enough room for the two of you as it is. I can provide you with a house with a garden where she can play…'

'And you think that's all it takes to make a child happy, do you, Marco? A house and a garden?' She laughed scornfully, hiding her pain beneath a layer of contempt. She wouldn't let him see how devastated she felt, couldn't bear him to know how foolish she was. She had actually thought that he was asking her to marry him because he wanted to spend his life with *her*!

'No, but I am sure it helps. Children don't take

kindly to being constantly uprooted. If we get married we can find a place where we can create a proper home for her, somewhere big enough to accommodate all her needs as she grows up.'

'And where do you suggest we do that? Here in London or in Italy? You seem to have everything worked out, Marco, so do tell me your plans.'

He frowned where he heard the edge in her voice. 'That is something we shall both have to decide. I am not proposing to ride roughshod over your wishes, if that's what you're implying. My sole concern is Lily and making sure that she has the very best start in life. It's obvious that you are a wonderful mother to her but I can give you both the security you need. You won't have to struggle to make ends meet any more.'

'So Lily gets a house with a garden and I get a free meal ticket for life? That's very generous, Marco.'

He stared arrogantly back at her. 'Providing for my child isn't an act of generosity.'

'No? Then I must be mistaken, obviously.' She stood up abruptly, unable to take any more. His cold-hearted proposal simply proved how little he really felt for her. Marco was prepared to do the right thing by providing for his daughter, and marrying her was merely part of the deal. If he had come out and stated that he had no feelings for her, he couldn't have made his position any clearer.

'I'm sorry, Marco, but I shall have to refuse your generous offer. Lily and I manage very well as we are. We don't need your help, thank you.'

'I have rights, too, Gina. I am Lily's father and I intend to make sure that she is properly cared for.'

'Which she is. She always will be, too, with or without your help, and preferably the latter.'

'I warn you, Gina, that if you try to stop me seeing her then I shall fight you.'

He stood up as well, looking so big and arrogant as he uttered his threats that she felt sick. How could she have misjudged the situation so badly? How had she seriously thought that he wanted to marry her because he loved her? Everything he had done, from ending their relationship three years ago to walking away that night they had been on the verge of making love, proved how little he cared about her. It was her own foolish heart that had made her want to believe he had changed.

'That's up to you, of course. I just hope that you'll remember what's important in all of this. Lily is the one who could get hurt, not you or me. But if that's a risk you are prepared to take, I can't stop you. Now I think it's time we left.'

She didn't give him a chance to reply as she fetched Lily. The little girl wasn't happy about having her fun cut short but Gina hardened her heart to her daughter's tears. This was for Lily's benefit, after all. She couldn't risk her precious child getting hurt even more when Marco tired of his role as the doting father.

She strapped Lily into her pushchair, refusing to listen to the insidious little voice that was whispering in her ear that it would be less likely to happen if they were married. There was no way she was marrying Marco, under any circumstances!

CHAPTER EIGHTEEN

THE following week was one of the most difficult of Marco's life. It was worse even than wak-
ing up in the back of that ambulance to find that
he had lost his memory. Gina refused to speak
to him about anything that didn't concern work.
The atmosphere in AAU whenever they were together was so bad, in fact, that he knew the rest
of the staff had noticed it. He racked his brain to
come up with a solution but there was nothing
he could do.

Gina had taken his marriage proposal entirely
the wrong way. He'd meant to help her, not hurt
her, yet that was what he had succeeded in doing.
If only he had admitted that it wasn't just for
Lily's sake that he wanted them to together, he
thought. Maybe he *had* tried to convince himself that it was a purely practical solution to their

problems, but in his heart he knew there'd been other reasons why he had proposed marriage to her. He wanted to be with Gina every bit as much as he wanted to be a good father to Lily, and the thought terrified him, made him see how vulnerable he was. Gina had an even bigger hold on him now than she'd had three years ago.

If Marco had thought things couldn't get any worse, he was mistaken. He was in the consultants' lounge when the phone rang. He picked up the receiver, surprised when an unfamiliar voice asked for him. His heart sank when the caller identified herself as the matron in charge of the nursing home where his grandmother lived. She briskly informed him that the old lady had pneumonia and was gravely ill. In the circumstances, he might wish to visit her.

Marco thanked her and hung up. He knew that he would never forgive himself if Nonna died without him being there, so he phoned round the airlines and managed to book himself a seat on a flight leaving that afternoon. Once he had informed the powers-that-be that he would need to take compassionate leave, he went to find Gina. Maybe she wouldn't be interested, but the very least he could do was to tell her that he would be away for a few days.

There was no sign of her on the unit and none of the staff seemed to know where she had gone either. He brushed aside Julie's offer to pass on a message and decided to phone her later instead. He certainly didn't want things to reach the point whereby they only communicated through a third party.

By the time he landed at Florence, it was already late but he phoned her mobile from the airport and left a message, briefly explaining what had happened when she failed to answer. Several times during the ensuing days he tried to contact her but without success. She was obviously screening his calls and it hurt to know that she didn't want to talk to him. He knew the situation couldn't continue and that he would have to do something about it when he returned to London. He wouldn't let her cut him out of his daughter's life. He couldn't bear it! He also couldn't bear the thought that she was cutting him out of her life too. Maybe it was a huge risk to allow himself to fall in love, he thought suddenly, but was it any worse than feeling like this, bereft and adrift?

Gina tried to keep everything normal for Lily's sake but it wasn't easy. The fact that Marco wasn't around should have helped but, strangely, it didn't. She missed him and there was no point denying it either.

It didn't help that Lily also seemed to miss him. When Gina suggested a visit to the park on the Saturday morning, the little girl eagerly demanded to know if Marco would be there. Gina gently explained that he'd had to go away but the ominous wobble to Lily's lower lip spoke volumes. It made her see that she couldn't cut him out of their lives, as she wanted to do. It wouldn't be fair to Lily. They would have to come to some sort of agreement to allow him access to their daughter, but that was all it would be—a civilised arrangement between two people for the benefit of their child. Marriage was strictly off the agenda!

Marco ended up staying almost a week in Florence as his grandmother fought off the effects of double pneumonia. Nobody expected her to pull through, himself included, but amazingly she defied all the odds. By the end of the week she was sitting up in bed, demanding her favourite food. He flew back to London early the following Friday and went straight into work and the first person he saw was Gina.

'Good morning,' he said, his heart leaping at the sight of her. He had missed her so much. She was such an important part of his life now that he simply couldn't imagine a future without her and didn't want to try. The thought shocked him so much that it was a moment before he realised that she was speaking. 'I'm sorry—what did you say?'

'I asked how your grandmother is.'

'I'm delighted to say that Nonna is much better.' He smiled at her. 'You obviously got my message, then?'

She shrugged. 'Yes.'

She didn't say anything else, certainly didn't explain why she had refused to answer his calls, and he didn't press her. The fact that she had bothered to enquire after his grandmother's health seemed a positive step and that was something to be grateful for.

'How's Lily?' he asked, following her to AAU.

'She's fine. Her spots have all gone now and she's back to her usual sunny self.'

'I missed her while I was away,' he said quietly.

She glanced at him and her expression softened. 'She missed you too, Marco. She was really disappointed when she found out you wouldn't be joining us at the park on Saturday.'

'Was she?' He put his hand on her arm and drew her to a halt. 'There has to be a way to work this out, Gina. I know I upset you the other day but I hope we can get past that—for Lily's sake.'

He knew he had said the wrong thing when her face immediately closed up. 'I'm sure we can reach some sort of agreement if we try. Now, if you'll excuse me, I need to get on.'

She hurried off down the ward, leaving him feeling more wretched than ever. He sighed as he headed to the consultants' lounge to find out what had been happening in his absence. If only he knew what Gina really wanted from him, it might help, but quite frankly he had no idea. Did she want him to be purely a father to their daughter or did she want more than that?

His heart leapt at the thought that she might want *him* before he battened it down. If he allowed himself to go down that route then he wouldn't be able to stop. Even now his mind was running riot, picturing how wonderful his life could be. He could have it all, a wife who loved him, a child they adored, the happily-ever-after that everyone dreamt of...

Until it all went wrong, of course.

Once again the old fears came rushing back and he knew that he couldn't do it. He was tempted, so tempted that it was agony not to follow his inclinations, yet the thought of going through all that pain again if anything happened was just too much. He couldn't bear it if he lost Gina as well.

Gina deliberately stayed out of Marco's way for the remainder of the morning. Maybe she was overreacting but did he have to constantly rub it in that he was only interested in their daughter? The thought played on her mind so that by the time she went to the canteen for lunch she had a headache brewing.

She took a couple of paracetamol then made her way back to AAU, using the stairs rather than the lift because she was early. She had just passed the barriers on the fourth floor when she heard someone shouting.

She stopped uncertainly, glancing along the empty corridor. Work on the roof had been put on hold while another structural report was prepared and there was nobody about. Had she imagined that noise or was there someone there?

She knew she had to check and slipped past the barriers. Huge metal props had been placed at intervals along the corridor to support the ceiling and she carefully skirted around them. She reached the door to the children's ward and peered inside but there was no sign of anyone so she carried on to Women's Surgical, gasping when she saw a teenage boy lying on the floor.

'What's happened?' she demanded, hurrying over to him.

'I tripped over and twisted my ankle.' He rubbed his eyes, obviously not wanting her to know that he had been crying. 'I think it's broken.'

'Let me have a look.' Gina knelt down and gently examined his ankle. 'It looks like it's broken to me, too. What are you doing here, though? Didn't you see the notices warning you to keep out?'

'I wanted to see what had happened to the roof,' he explained sheepishly, and she sighed.

'Well, you certainly got more than you bargained for.' She stood up. 'I'll have to phone for a porter. We'll need a wheelchair to get you out of here.'

Picking up the phone, she asked for a porter,

briefly explaining what had happened, and went back to the boy. 'My name's Gina, by the way. What's yours?'

'Richard.'

'Nice to meet you, Richard, although I wish the circumstances had been different.' She smiled when he rolled his eyes. 'How come you're in the hospital in the first place? Are you visiting someone?'

'No, I'm here with my dad. I'm supposed to be shadowing him while he works—it's some stupid idea my school came up with—but it's so boring.' He shrugged. 'Dad told me about the roof, so I thought I'd check it out.'

'I see. And who's your dad?'

'Tom Petty. He works in ED. Do you know him?'

Gina nodded. 'Yes, I know Tom. I don't think he's going to be too impressed by having you for a patient, though.'

Richard was about to say something when all of a sudden there was a rumbling noise above them. Gina gasped when she looked up and saw that the metal prop they were sitting next to had started to shift out of place.

'Look out!' she cried as a section of the ceiling suddenly gave way.

She threw herself on top of the boy, shielding him as chunks of plaster rained down on them. Something hit her on the head and in the final second before everything went black she found herself wishing that she had told Marco she loved him. Maybe he wouldn't want to hear it but all of a sudden it seemed important that he should know the truth.

Marco was dealing with a new admission when he became aware of a commotion in the ward. He looked up, frowning when he saw Julie clap her hand over her mouth. It was obvious that something had happened so he quickly excused himself and went to see what was wrong.

'It's Gina.' There were tears in Julie's eyes as she turned to him. 'She's been hurt.'

'Hurt?'

'Yes. Another section of the roof has caved in

and it appears that Gina was there when it happened. They've managed to get her out and taken her to ED…'

Marco didn't wait to hear anything else. He'd heard more than enough as it was. Gina was hurt and he had to get to her! He ran out of AAU and straight along the corridor to ED. 'You've got Gina Lee in here. Where is she?' he demanded when he reached the nursing station.

'Resus,' the nurse replied, but she was speaking to fresh air. Marco had already gone.

He raced to Resus, his heart hammering as he pushed open the door. Only the most severely injured patients were treated in here and the thought that Gina fell into that category was more than he could bear. He scanned the room, oblivious to the startled looks he was attracting from the staff. He didn't care what anyone thought. He only cared about Gina. He needed to see her and make sure she was all right…

His gaze suddenly alighted on a figure lying on the end bed and his heart turned over when he realised it was her. She looked so small and defenceless as she lay there with all the various tubes and leads attached to her body. Marco felt a wave of ice-cold fear pass over him. It took every scrap of courage he could muster to cross the room.

'How is she?' he asked, staring down at her. Her eyes were closed and there was a huge purple bruise on her forehead but apart from that, she appeared uninjured.

'Not too bad,' Simon Rutherford, the senior registrar, replied cheerfully. 'A chunk of the ceiling hit her on the head so she may have a concussion. No fractures, though, and it doesn't appear that there are any internal injuries, although we can't rule them out just yet. All in all, I'd say she was extremely lucky. It's not every day that you have half a ton of ceiling fall on top of you and live to tell the tale!'

Simon moved away, leaving Marco alone with her. He reached for her hand, his own hand trembling as he raised it to his lips. He had been so scared, so terrified that he would lose her, and yet the worst thing of all had been the thought that he hadn't told her how much he loved her. He had been a coward, denying his feelings, turning his back on love because he'd been afraid, but he wouldn't make that mistake again.

'Marco?'

The sound of her voice brought his eyes winging to her face and he felt joy fill him when he saw the way she was looking at him. Bending, he kissed her on the mouth, feeling his joy intensify when she kissed him back. He drew back, knowing that she could see exactly how he felt but he didn't care. He was past lying to her or to himself. He loved her and he wanted her to know that.

'I love you, Gina,' he said simply.

'And I love you too, Marco.' She smiled into his eyes. 'There, I've said it, so if another chunk of ceiling drops on me then at least I've told you the truth.'

He laughed. 'You have and believe me it's the best thing I've heard for a very long time.'

'Is it? Are you sure about that?' Her gaze was searching and he sighed.

'Yes, I'm sure. It's taken me a long to admit how I feel but now that I have, I am not going to change my mind. I love you, *tesoro*, and I love the fact that you love me.'

'Good. It will make life a whole lot simpler, don't you think?' She gave a little chuckle. 'This isn't how I imagined it would be when I told you.'

'Oh, so you were planning on making your confession *before* the accident happened?' He smiled at her. 'That sets my mind at rest.'

'It does?'

'Mmm. I was afraid the bump on your head might have had something to do with it.'

'It may have done,' she replied saucily. 'A bump on the head can cause a lot of strange things to happen to a person.'

'As I know from experience.' He dropped another kiss on her lips. 'If I hadn't had that bump on my head, I would never have met you again.'

'Do you think it was fate intervening?'

'I don't know. But whatever it was, I am truly grateful.' He pressed her hand against his heart. 'I found the love of my life and my daughter.'

'I'm sorry that I never tried harder to tell you about Lily,' she began, but he shushed her.

'No. That's all in the past and it doesn't matter now. You did what you thought was best and I don't blame you after the way I'd behaved. I was such a coward, Gina, and I shall always regret that. I missed out on three years of happiness because I was afraid of falling in love with you.'

'So it wasn't just because you didn't love me as much as Francesca?' she asked in a small voice, and he stared at her in surprise.

'No! That was never an issue. Oh, I loved Francesca, but my feelings for her have nothing to do with how I feel about you. I love you with every scrap of my being and all I want is to spend the rest of my life with you so I can prove it to you.'

'You don't have to prove anything to me, Marco.' Her eyes glistened with tears as she reached up to pull his head down so she could kiss him. 'I believe you because I love you, because I know you wouldn't lie to me about something as important as this.'

'I wouldn't.' They kissed hungrily, a kiss that would have lasted a lot longer if they hadn't been interrupted.

'Sorry to break things up, folks, but Gina is booked in for a scan.' Tom Petty grinned at them. 'You can resume what you were doing afterwards with my blessing. In fact, I shall personally find you some place private where you won't be interrupted. I owe you, Gina, for what you did for my son.'

Marco wasn't sure what Tom meant by that but didn't ask. No doubt Gina would explain it all to him later. He moved away from the bed as the porters arrived to take her to radiology. 'I'd better get back to AAU, I suppose. They'll be wondering where I've got to.'

'Oh, don't worry about that.' Tom grinned at him. 'No doubt the jungle drums will be spreading the news even as we speak.'

'The news?' Marco repeated.

'About you and Gina... I am right, aren't I? I mean, you two are an item?'

Marco laughed. 'If you mean are we together

then, yes, we are.' He captured her hand and kissed it. 'We are very much together and intend to stay that way.'

'Good stuff! I love a happy ending.' Tom sketched them a wave and hurried off to deal with a new patient.

Marco turned to Gina. 'I'll be back as soon as I can, my darling. Promise.'

'I'm not going anywhere,' she replied, loving him with her eyes.

The porters took over then, wheeling her out of Resus. Marco followed although it felt as though his feet weren't touching the floor as he made his way to AAU. He was floating on Cloud Nine, hovering in his own little world, a world filled with love and happiness.

He pushed open the door, his head whirling with everything that had happened in the past half-hour. His life had changed completely. Now he had a future to look forward to, a whole new life that he had never dreamt he would have. He felt so lucky to have been given a second chance, knew that he would do everything possible to make sure that nothing went wrong, but he wouldn't waste the coming years, fearing what they held in store. He had wasted enough time doing that and now he intended to enjoy every second. He, Gina and Lily would create some wonderful new memories. Together.

EPILOGUE

FLORENCE lay serene and beautiful under a cloudless blue sky. It was the middle of June and the weather was perfect. Gina smiled as she stepped in front of the mirror and studied her reflection.

It was her wedding day and the dress she had chosen was everything she had dreamt it would be. Made from a length of antique cream lace that Marco's beloved grandmother had given her, it fell in soft folds to her ankles. It was a dream of a dress and she loved it, knew that Marco would love it too.

Happiness welled up inside her as she thought about what had happened in the past few months. She and Lily had moved out of their flat into Marco's apartment. Although Gina had been worried at first about how Lily would cope with the new arrangements she had settled in immediately. The little girl seemed to accept that Marco was part of their life now and obviously enjoyed being with him. Although they hadn't told her yet that he was her father, Gina was sure that Lily would take that in her stride too when the time came. There was already a bond between them, which was growing stronger with every day that passed.

Once the move had been accomplished they had arranged their wedding. When Marco had asked her if she would consider getting married in Florence so his grandmother could be there, she had agreed at once. She knew how important family was to Marco and wanted the day to be as special for him as it was for her.

Everything had gone surprisingly smoothly. Not even the fact that she had been summoned to appear at the board of inquiry the week before had spoiled things. She knew that she hadn't done anything wrong and in the event that had been proved when fresh evidence had been presented.

Engineers investigating the reason why the prop had failed had checked back through the

CCTV footage on the days leading up to the accident and discovered that Miles had been in the vicinity. He had been asked to explain what he'd been doing there and eventually admitted that he had gone there to alter the notes he had retrieved from Theatre. He was currently suspended and it looked likely that he would be dismissed. Maybe Gina should have felt angry about the way Miles had tried to lay the blame on her but, quite frankly, it didn't seem to matter. She was going to marry the man she loved and nothing was more important than that!

A soft knock at the door made her turn and she smiled when she saw Marco come into the bedroom. They had decided to walk to the village church together. Maybe it wasn't traditional for the bride and groom to arrive together but after being apart for so long, every second they were apart seemed a waste. Now she felt a thrill run through her when he stopped and stared at her.

'You look beautiful, *cara*,' he said, his deep voice throbbing with a passion that made her shudder. He crossed the room and took her hand so that he could press a kiss against her palm. 'I cannot believe that in a short while you will be my wife.'

'Believe it, Marco, because it's going to happen!'

She reached up and kissed him softly on the lips, feeling the tremor that ran through him. Marco was unable to hide how he felt about her these days. Every touch, every kiss, drew a reaction from him as they did from her. It was proof she no longer needed of how much he loved her.

She stepped back and smiled at him. 'Is Lily all right?'

'She's fine, very excited about being a flower girl.' He laughed wryly. 'She's practising throwing her rose petals. I left Nonna in charge but I cannot see her stopping her. Lily can twist Nonna round her little finger, can't she? I only hope there are some petals left by the time we get to church!'

Gina laughed. 'We can only hope for the best.'

'It doesn't matter even if the basket is empty. Nothing is going to spoil today, is it?'

'No. It's going to be the best day of my life, Marco.'

'Mine too,' he murmured, bending so he could kiss her. 'But the most wonderful thing of all is knowing that we have a whole future to look forward to.'

Gina closed her eyes as she let the magic sweep her away. She was so lucky, lucky to have found Marco again, lucky to have his child, lucky to be loved by the man she adored. The future couldn't have been any better!

* * * * *